We met in Cape Town

Ian R Gale

For all those I really did meet in Cape Town.

*This novel is entirely a work of fiction.
The names, characters and incidents portrayed in it are
the work of the author's imagination*

We met in Cape Town

Prologue

Beyond the vast openness of the Atlantic Ocean, the setting sun majestically, unceremoniously lays to rest another day. The cool April breeze whistles through the bushes and delicately brushes the calm, cold, dark water, collecting scent, salt, and moisture, and brings it to their faces. On the rocks of Bakoven beach a flurry of air swirls between their bodies, around them, binding them; seven souls, together again, like one as never before.

'We had some fun times, eh?'
'For sure, but what a fucking mess.'
'Good times.'
'Did we bring wine?... Just asking.'
'We don't have glasses.'
'It's never stopped him before.'

Against the relentlessly evolving autumnal sunset, seven friends circle the pale flickering light of a cheap white candle. Each one in their own way says goodbye. The sun sets, ashes are sprinkled in the breeze into the ocean, the flame is snuffed.

'Now, where's the bar?'

Marie

'If you wanna make one million bucks in this town, start with ten million then open a restaurant.' She still remembers the whimsical yet salient advice from Tony, who owns one of the most successful restaurants in Cape Town. Successful, not necessarily due to exceedingly fantastic food or memorable dining experiences, but more from sheer hard work, a few savvy connections, and smart decisions. Tony's advice, whilst a little 'tongue-in-cheek', was not to discourage, more to caution. All the same, Marie remembers how she was inspired.

She sits on the rocks near the sandy beach looking out into the cold, still water. She is tired of the restaurant, and tired of maintaining her facade. For all these years here, most of her friends knew very little about her, why she is in Cape Town, or anything relating to her previous life, which suits her fine. It's just becoming exhausting. For Marie, her friends are her saving grace in a complex situation. She has shared more than one drink on more than one occasion with them all, which has been sufficient familiarity. Except that now she feels the need to 'come clean' with a few of them, and let them into her life. *Peu à peu.*

-§-

The wind. 'Fock!' As Marie stands outside the commercial property for rent on Kloof Street with a perfect view of Table Mountain, the wind, like so many days this week, is ferocious, cyclonic. *It's normal,* she concedes.
'Sorry, I'm a little late.'
A little, Marie thinks in exasperation, checking her petite Cartier wristwatch just a little too demonstrably.
'Ag maan, shame, this wind, it just picked up,' the overly groomed realtor says, dressed in a light grey, above-the-knee skirt and matching, one-size-too-small jacket, walking uneasily in her puce stilettos, which should have

been reserved only for a wedding reception in the eastern suburbs, frantically rummaging through her fake Gucci handbag to find the keys of the empty restaurant. 'Marie? Rebecca. Nice to meet you.'

'Enchantée,' Marie replies, elongating the salutation, and immediately hating the sound of her native tongue in such an encounter, and the (perhaps) unintended condescending overtone it presents. She knows she is not that person, but realtors bring out the worst in her, and old habits die hard. Once upon a time she would have had no reason to meet with such a person, leaving it to her husband's PA to deal with all this unpleasant blether.

'It comes with a fully equipped "commercial" kitchen, mindlessly making quotation marks with two fingers in the air, with her long fingers, finished with mother-of-pearl lacquered nails, to emphasise the implication of 'commercial'. 'There's a double fridge but no freezer. I guess you can get one later. All the crockery, cutlery, and glassware are here, all the tables and chairs are staying, the fireplace is fully operational, although it might need a bit of a clean. Food stock and bar inventory will be your responsibility, of course. The previous restaurateur is happy to put you in touch with distributors if you need that.'

'Thank you, I have contacts already.'

'The permit allows for seating in these little alcoves at the front, but not on the footpath.'

'Aha.'

Nervously, Rebecca thinks it important to begin adding more pedestrian information about serviettes and tablecloths, but is stopped short by Marie's hand gesture. Rebecca notices the ring. *That rock!*

'I get the idea,' Marie assures. 'Let's do this. Where do I sign?'

-§-

Serge's has been open for some time, and Marie is committed to making it work. She has to. She did nothing to improve the interior of the place. It's fine: the food would speak for itself. The restaurant had lost its uninterrupted view of Table Mountain to a new development across the road - all in the name of progress. Marie remembers Rebecca mentioning something about it and adding 'A view is a privilege, not a right.' But at that stage Marie had already dismissed Rebecca and had decided on the property.

C'est la vie, Marie thinks, sitting on the small balcony of her apartment, not very far from the restaurant. Glass of Krug Grande Cuvée in hand, she savours this short moment of peace. From her balcony, there is no view, and little wind. It's a tranquil place, a haven; there is no staff asking inane questions again about how to sauté the parboiled broccoli the way she likes it to be done - with real butter and a little fresh garlic, never minced with those anathema kitchen appliances, rather squashed and finely diced. 'It's not rocket science' she finds herself reiterating to the cook! 'And if you ask me how to make mayonnaise again, you're fired.' Despite it all, she does love living in Cape Town, her new home. Work is intense in the restaurant, and the hours long. Her brother Pierre has proved himself to be next to useless in the restaurant, perhaps more than the hired staff. *So much for a family business.* It was his choice to be like he is, and it's too late to change now. Some customers even avoid coming in if they see him waiting tables. 'I'll have to let him go. It makes more sense not having him around me all the time,' Marie mutters to herself after taking another sip of champagne. Part of her fear is, however, that he knows too much about her previous life, and she feels unable to fully trust him - to trust any man. She will always, of course, be extremely appreciative of his support and sheltering presence when she scarpered from Lille. Without Pierre, it would have been impossible to escape the controlling, overbearing, and violent clutches of her husband. Lucien is the reason she decided never to go back to France, to Europe. He would find her there.

Marie looks at her watch, remembering the gift to herself on their 5th wedding anniversary. God knows she received so few gifts from Lucien on birthdays, anniversaries, Christmas, and as time went on, she didn't expect any. It was only right she remember such a momentous occasion - good or bad - with something more valuable than their relationship. 'Fock! Is that the time?' She downs the last of the champagne, places the glass in the dishwasher, grabs her bag and heads out the door. *I'll have to drive, it's too far to walk now.*

The new, black VW Polo turns right onto Long Street. One-way traffic enables her to stay in the right lane, which has always felt more natural for Marie, and she heads straight through the robots onto Kloof. *I'll turn onto Union - should be able to find a park there.* Making the turn left onto Union Street, the Polo somewhat absentmindedly takes the right lane again, heading straight toward the oncoming old Datsun Sunny. Brakes screech. 'FOCK!'

A rather petite female driver is facing Marie, clearly talking to herself - a bit in shock, Marie assumes - but smiling and gazing out of her windscreen as if searching for answers.

For a moment, with the two cars facing each other, Marie continues to stare blankly out of her windscreen in disbelief. The world stops and the passers-by, wildly gesticulating and shouting, are in slow motion and silent: a defense mechanism she developed to blockout the verbal abuse during arguments she had on a daily basis with Lucien. The increasing sound of a car horn drags her back into reality.

'You gonna move ya car, lady? Or stay there all day?' An impatient, stocky, well-tanned, young Afrikaner, wearing a white singlet and an Adidas cap, shouts from the driver's side window of his Bakkie. Marie can only assume his questions are rhetorical, and she turns to look at him, over the top of her Ray-Bans, with a level of disdain.

'I gotta move m' bakkie, and you take the park.'

More collected now, Marie checks, drives forward, the Bakkie leaves behind her, and she reverses into his park. The Sunny has gone. Marie gets out of her car and instinctively, as she locks the car with the remote, heads toward the car park at the rear of the shopping centre, almost bumping into a delicate lady with auburn hair, immaculately set in a bob, and wearing a comfortable, floral summer dress, and 'sensible' shoes, who emerged from the small set of stairs leading up to Union Street.

'I'm so sorry,' Marie confesses. 'My head was elsewhere, too many years of driving in France.'

'That's fine - that was almost twice, bumping into each other,' chirps the lady.

'Are you OK?'

'I'm fine. It could have been a lot worse. Just as well I'm a slow driver.' She giggles a little, nervously.

'Really, I'm so sorry.'

'It's fine, really. It got my heart racing again...good for the immune system.'

'Listen, I own the restaurant across the street. Let me get you a coffee, or tea, or something stronger. I insist.'

'Well, who can say no to a nice cup of tea? I'm Rachel.'

'Marie.'

A few customers are in the restaurant, some regulars and a couple of new guys in the front alcove. Marie nods politely to them both, who seem to be in completely different worlds from each other, one simply drinking a glass of red wine and the other checking his phone. She ensures Rachel is seated and comfortable in the opposite side alcove and that she has the order correct: English Breakfast Tea, apparently Twinings is OK, before striding off to check on the staff. She returns with the tea - milk but no sugar. Marie sits down next to Rachel, and one of the staff brings her an espresso.

Marie takes a sip of her coffee, and looks at Rachel. Such a kind, open face. She suspects she's around 50, and looks good, but her auburn hair is too neat, and Marie realises it's a wig. 'So, what do you do here?'

Rachel puts down the teacup, with an expression of sincere enjoyment of the tea. 'I own a small guesthouse. Been doing it for years now. Originally from the UK, you probably guessed that, you know, with my plum accent and all,' she giggles, 'but now I am very comfortable in this beautiful city. I have made a lot of new friends, and I seriously don't think I'll ever be moving back, certainly not for a very long time, if at all.' She picks up the teacup again, holding it with two hands and continues, 'Cape Town has everything you need: It's a beautiful city, and quite safe. You can still see a play or musical; there is even an opera company here. I mean, I'm not really into opera, perhaps a bit of Gilbert and Sullivan, but it's good to know you can go if you want to, and there's the Cape Philharmonic Orchestra! The hospitals and medical services are world class, there is plenty of very good food and wine, and some fabulous restaurants. It seems very easy to make friends... I have made plenty of new friends, oh... I think I said that.' She sips some tea, and smiles. 'To be honest, and you know, we have just met, but I really feel there is no life for me back in the UK. After my husband died, I decided to make a clean break and start a new life somewhere.' Another sip. 'I sold everything we had in Brighton and started over here. Bought a cute little guesthouse and have made a lot of new friends.' Another silent moment, as Rachel stares blankly and smiles. 'What about you..?'

Marie smiles warmly, and winks at her. 'Oh, I would be delighted to be your new friend.'

They laugh a little and take several sips of their beverage and enjoy a moment's silence.

'Thank you for the tea. I think I might have been a bit more shaken than I had thought, so the tea has been most beneficial. Now, I need to run along and tend to some errands, but may I leave you my contact details? Perhaps we could catch up sometime for lunch or whatever.' Rachel finds a card in her purse. 'I met a gorgeous young couple quite a few months ago. They're very attractive. He's a real stunner, if you know what I mean.' She bumps her elbow into Marie's arm. 'He's English - from London I believe - and she's Irish - "to-be-sure, to-be-sure,"' she giggles. 'They have also invested in a guesthouse here - much more upmarket than mine. They both enjoy the finer things in life, so I must tell them I've found this fabulous restaurant... open for lunch? or dinner...?' She states as a question looking to Marie quizzically.

'We are open for breakfast, lunch, and dinner, and everything in between.' Marie confirms with a warm smile.

'That's perfect. Then for sure you will see me again, and hopefully you can meet... um, their names... William and Annie. Thank you again for the tea, and it is a pleasure to meet you, Marie. Must rush.' Rachel stands and Marie follows suit. As a natural gesture, Rachel gives Marie a kiss on each cheek to say goodbye. Marie goes to kiss a third time, a practice she willingly adopted from her Dutch friends, but Rachel is already collecting her bag. She gives Marie a business card and heads for the door, waving cheerily to the two guys in the alcove as she glides out as if on air.

How charming, Marie thinks, smiling and looking down at the business card Rachel left her. *Rachel Palmer, Freedom House.*

Marie collects the teacup and saucer and the espresso cup and walks to the back of the restaurant toward the kitchen, still smiling. Pushing through the café doors with her back into the kitchen, she notices one of the guys in the alcove has left the restaurant soon after Rachel. *Interesting.*

Good! No questions from the staff! Plates, glasses, cutlery have been collected and washing is being done. Effectively it's the end of lunch service. She returns to the restaurant, and immediately the gentleman in the alcove gestures for the bill. Marie slides behind the bar and accesses the information on the POS system. All seems to be in order: one chopped salad, one chicken korma, and a bottle of Hartenberg cabernet sauvignon. She prints the bill, slips it into a leather wallet, and brings it to the table. 'Everything to your liking, sir?'

'Fabulous,' he replies. 'Très agréable,' he adds. Marie smiles but says nothing. He continues, 'I like it here; it's the second time we have been and I like it a lot. The first time we had a male waiter.'

'... and your friend, are you together?' Marie asks boldly.

'We are as together as any two people could possibly be... under the circumstances,' he replies, looking at Marie with a devilish sparkle in his eye and a grin. 'Excuse me, but we couldn't help eavesdropping on your conversation with... is it Rachel? Certainly after watching you nearly drive into the front of her,' he says with a smirk. 'It seems all immigrants in this town either own a restaurant or a guesthouse. And we are no different, having just recently purchased and renovated one in Oranjezicht. Our first year of trading.'

'Is that a restaurant, or a guesthouse?' Marie inquires.

He smiles wryly, 'No need to worry, my dear - it's a guesthouse. We are Montrose Manor. Now, not only will we be back for lunch nearly every day, but we will also advise our guests to come here for their first meal to find their bearings.'

'Thank you so much,' Marie says with gratitude. 'Then I'm sure we can find a way to scratch each other's back.'

'You see, this is one of the reasons you and I are going to be great friends.' He smiles and winks. 'I'm Ayden.'

'Marie.'

'And him, what's plodding back in here, is Daniel.'

Daniel comes back into the restaurant, a little out of breath, and sees them both staring at him. 'What?'

'This is Marie. French, I believe, or am I mistaking the accent?' Ayden says pryingly.

'Oui, tu as raison, enchantée.' Marie offers her hand to Daniel.

Daniel delicately takes her fingers in his hand and mock kisses the dorsal of her hand. 'A great pleasure to meet you, Marie. We like your restaurant. We have a guesthou...'

'Done all that!' Ayden interrupts abruptly.

Daniel huffs.

Marie smiles at Ayden's faux impatience with Daniel. It is clear to see that the two of them are in love, despite any bravado from Ayden. Marie learned very quickly, and first hand, what public displays of serious annoyance looks and feels like. There is no mistaking it, and this was not that.

'Right, time to go. I'll fill you in on the way home,' he says to Daniel. He turns to Marie and smiles. 'Nice to meet you again Marie, and we will see you soon. Oh, by the way, your male waiter... don't mean to be rude, but he could do with some more training.'

They head out the door. Ayden had paid with cash and included a most generous tip.

Marie smiles as she walks behind the bar. Not because of the generous tip, but because, increasingly, she feels like she is home in Cape Town.

The restaurant took up most of her time, but it did afford her the opportunity to meet new people. With the exception of Pierre, she had trained her staff well, allowing her to get away for a couple of days mid-week to relax and enjoy the trappings of the Western Cape. What she couldn't find to enjoy, however, was a man! It seemed she only met gay guys in Cape Town. *That has to change*, she thinks as she pours herself a glass of wine behind the bar. As much as she hated to think about it, she missed the sex with Lucien, which remains the most incredible part of a perverted, sadistic relationship. *Where do I find a hot, single, straight guy in this town?* She downs her wine and heads into the kitchen.

Two or three months after meeting Rachel, Marie met William and Annie. They had come into Serge's on Rachel's recommendation, for which Marie had thanked her on the several occasions they had caught up. For Marie, both William and Annie are very charming people, old world European for such a young couple, and both very attractive. What's more, William - Bill - is not just attractive; he has a sensuality that makes her go weak at the knees. He is an extremely strapping man; fit, ruggedly handsome, well-built and sensibly muscular, you know, without being grotesque, bright blue eyes, and wavy dark blonde hair. Marie smiles. *I hardly noticed him at all.* She often fantasised about having sex with Bill, and wondered whether he did the same about her. When they first met in the restaurant, Marie accosted herself, realising that she was already starting to flirt with Bill, a somewhat automatic reaction for her, and apparently for Bill as well. Annie, in a natural and a kind-hearted way brought them both back to reality by asking for a bottle of wine.

Annie adored Bill, not because of his looks. It was clearly much deeper than that. Additionally, her adoration was unquestionably reciprocated by Bill. She was petite but not wasted. Fit-ish, certainly in shape, but Marie got the impression that, with everything in Annie's life, if she couldn't be bothered with it, it didn't happen. That included workouts, and people. Neither of them were fussy, but they did expect good service, good wine, and good food. No doubt they enjoyed the finer things in life, travelling between their home in London and their second home in Cape Town.

Marie steps into Serge's late morning, just a few minutes later than she had intended and heads for the kitchen. She tries not to stare at the two new guys busy on their laptops, sitting on the bench along the wall closest to the kitchen, most probably because there are power outlets. The only two customers, each with only a coffee, and each 'clicking' away, one on a black MacBook, the other on a Dell. About her age, she guesses, one particularly handsome, with short brown hair, chiseled jawline, 'designer stubble', and broad shoulders. European for sure... and gay! *What is it about this fucking town that attracts so many gay guys? Or is it just me?*
Marie walks from the kitchen and approaches the table 'Anything more I can get for you gentlemen?'
'Not at the moment.' The handsome one says. Looking up to Marie with his hazel eyes, 'We love your restaurant. I'm guessing you're the owner.'
'Oui.'
'Hi, I'm Kris.'
'Marie.' She extends her hand and they shake. 'Hmm, I'm guessing either Belgian or Nederlander.'
Kris smiles, a little surprised. 'Dutch, correct - Limburg, Maastricht. At least you didn't say German!' He winks, 'And I'm guessing from France or southern Belgium.'
'France, yes, from Lille... years ago now.'
'Ah, we were practically neighbours.'
'Hi, I'm Ivan.' Breaking into the conversation. 'We were walking past and noticed this beautiful café - with tablecloths, no less. So we had to come in.'
Marie smiles. 'Well, it's almost lunch service, so tablecloths are essential. Your accent I can't pick. Not UK?'
'Yes, not UK.' Ivan smirks 'It's a good Australian blend. At least you didn't say New Zealand.' He winks.

Marie stares at him for just a moment, *weird joke*. 'Are you guys travelling, on holiday?'

Kris takes the lead, 'We bought a guesthouse last year on holiday here...'

'As you do.' Marie jests, already forming opinions about the two of them, and concocting her own story. As Kris continues talking, she thinks she sees Pierre walk past the restaurant on the other side of the street with a male companion, but her view is blocked by her waitress coming out from behind the bar. *Why would he not come in?* she thinks.

'...it was called 'The Lady Victoria', it's in Gardens, just a short walk from here. After we... both had to go... Hong Kong and Berlin...'

Marie's not fully listening, but tries hard to look interested as she distractedly tries to see past her staff. *That's not Pierre! Wait!*

'... So we need to get... dust and disasters out of our heads.' Kris concludes.

Silence! Marie returns her attention to her new guests, smiling.

Ivan adds 'So we have just officially moved to Cape Town to live.'

'Another guesthouse couple. Sorry,' still trying to get back to the conversation, 'I assume a couple.'

Two nods.

She collects her thoughts and dismisses the distraction of seeing Pierre. 'Well, you have a lot of people to meet. Guesthouse owners are coming out of our ears in this town. I think the looming World Cup has drawn them out of the woodwork. All lovely people - well, the people I know at least. And that's all that matters. I'll introduce you to them all.'

'Fantastic. We look forward to it.' Ivan says with enthusiasm. 'Now, let's have a look at the wine list for lunch.'

-§-

Marie had learned to read people more accurately, and successfully, since 'falling in love' with Lucien. She is more than confident that her new friends, despite differences in countries and cultures, will all get on famously. There is no pretense in any of them, and they all like wine, which is always going to help. Nevertheless, as much as she loves meeting new expats, it is always bitter-sweet for Marie. Unlike other foreigners, Marie knew she could never call Europe home again. It's not regret, or jealousy, or animosity toward them, rather a grieving of the life she lost. She misses the glorious north French winters, the radiantly clear days and the glistening white blanket of snow, the coldness, ice skating. She misses the spectacular changes in season - changes that are evident in temperature and scenery and apparel. As much as she really enjoys summer in Cape Town, it could not replace the aroma of summer, and the vibrant blue sky, in France. For sure she misses the lifestyle Lucien and she had enjoyed - the trappings of wealth - the 'things' she could buy, their home, the furniture, the concerts, the holidays, the art, the clothes, meeting important and famous people. It's all gone, save a few pieces she grabbed from her private dressing room: a few dresses, her beautiful ring, a watch, and a photo of the two of them at the Cannes Film Festival in an antique photo frame, before rushing out via the fire escape of their penthouse in Vieux-Lille. It could get her down if she let it. But she is strong.

-§-

When Marie receives an invitation to the gala opening of Kris and Ivan's guesthouse, she smiles. An ideal opportunity to don a party dress and heels, and let her hair down. It's been such a long time since she has attended a real gala, and this seemed like the next best thing. The manager of the Victoria Boutique Villa, who issued the invitation, also asked if Marie could extend the invitation to Pierre. A bit tacky, she thought, that the manager was incapable of inviting him personally. In any case, Marie chose not to tell Pierre and instead enjoy a night of anonymity.

It's a lovely cool evening, no wind, perfect. Marie parks along Kelvin Street closest to Kloof Nek, demurely steps out of her car in her black cocktail dress and black heels. She locks the car and walks down toward the guesthouse, flicking her long, free, dark hair behind her shoulders.

Once inside the garden, she stands for a few minutes looking at the beautiful house. *Nice job, boys,* she thinks to herself as she grabs a glass of champagne. She is naturally drawn to the kitchen to see if she can assist with something... perhaps more likely, thinking that she will need to fix a few common errors in catering. No sooner had she found the kitchen than Kris found her. He leads her to the veranda and they chat for a short time. She has an instinctual fondness for Kris; his looks, his confidence, and genuine warmth, but she is also aware that the conversation is beginning to be an inquisition. Tonight she just wants to enjoy the champagne, the house, and mindless conversation.

To her delight Ivan interrupts, 'Rachel, can I introduce you to Marie?'

'Marie!' Rachel says with surprise. 'We know each other. It's a village here.' She says to Ivan.

Marie notices Kris leaving and smiles. *There'll be plenty of time for questions later, Kris.*

'Then I don't need to tell you that Marie owns one of the best restaurants in Cape Town.' Ivan declares. 'But Marie, darling, and this may be the champagne talking, you have to do something with Pierre! He is no asset to your restaurant.'

Marie tunes out as Ivan and Rachel continue chatting. Looking at Rachel's simple dress and flat shoes, she thinks, *I need to help you with a makeover.* Then, focusing on Ivan's drunken comment, she sighs, *Pierre.* Of course he is right, but she knows Pierre better than anyone, and how much in debt she is to him. She smiles reservedly, 'In due course.'

'Who's for a top-up?' Ivan says, then stops to look into the street, somewhat distractedly, then drunkenly turns and heads toward the house to find champagne. Marie looks behind her into Bath Street. *Is that Ayden and Daniel in their car?*

The Wednesday Lunch Club was initiated by Marie not long after William and Annie had a braai for a bunch of friends at their house, which she was unable to attend because of work. Perhaps that was the final nail in her 'I have no life' coffin. The concept was supposed to be a reconnaissance outing for the guesthouse owners, but for her, it was a chance to get out of the restaurant and her small apartment, and to be with her friends. Her mid-week country escapes were becoming a little dull on her own, so she needed to get out of her routine, even for a lunch once a week, and, if she were honest, she created another opportunity to flirt with William.

Fundamentally the club works well, but she is one of the team of eight who can't resist a good drink on her day off, which often doesn't end attractively. She smirks a little with embarrassment, remembering the day she made a waitress cry, all over a tip, which wasn't significant enough for the poor girl. She feels a little proud that her idea has become a solid institution with her friends. It's been a staple social event for them, on-and-off for a couple of years, but now with the emphasis on just getting together regularly. Whenever enough people are available on Wednesday, and/or because someone has discovered yet another interesting place to eat. However, for Marie, the lunch club ultimately becomes impossible; any social outing is difficult for her. She just can't leave the safety of her apartment or the restaurant. Panic and fear are festering in her, and she is increasingly unable to control it.

-§-

Of all the events that weaved in society, or personally surrounded Marie and her friends in the years they were together, none affected her more than that single event in February 2013. Marie, in her apartment, is in shock. A whole nation halts in disbelief. A cold sweat of panic and remembrance, and the fear comes rushing back to her. This single event is the strongest confirmation of her decision to get out of Lille and never go back. Paralympian Oscar Pistorius has shot and killed his fiancé Reeva Steenkamp, in cold blood; shots explode through a door as she hides in fear inside a locked bathroom. The violence, the unimaginable hatred, the anger, the sickening macho culture - it's all too familiar, and Marie was a lucky one. Reeva was not. Fuck you Oscar, and fuck you Lucien.

The following morning, Marie wakes up in a pool of sweat, shaking in fear and disbelief. She can't believe how affected she is by the Pistorius story, that the gut-wrenching fear has returned. She has to talk to someone - a friend, not Pierre. She calls Ayden on his mobile.

Ayden

'We should have brought a torch. These rocks are treacherous after sunset,' Ayden declares with the troupe behind him. 'There are plenty of bars along the Promenade in Camps Bay.'

'We can't stay, Ayden, we have to pack up the house and pack ourselves for our early flight tomorrow morning.' William says, as he gently leads Annie by her arm in the right direction over the rocks.

'A pity.' Ayden looks at Bill, 'Oh for fuck's sake, just pick her up in your big arms and carry her to the road... What about the rest of you lot?'

'I'm up for cheeky red,' Ivan hollers.

'When are you never!'

The seven friends reach the car park at Bakoven. Rachel wipes a tear from her eye, and Daniel puts his arm around her shoulders, bringing her into a side embrace and rubs her upper arm, typically for Daniel, an action somewhere between a serious full on hug, and nothing at all.

Kris is the last to arrive, urn still in his hand. 'What do I do with this?' Holding up the empty pot.

'I'd like to keep it if that's Ok with everyone,' Rachel offers. There is a general murmur of acceptance amongst the group. 'Can I grab a ride back to town with you two?' She looks at William and Annie. Annie nods.

'Right, just the four of us then.' Ayden says, on a mission to get to Camps Bay.

Ivan turns to say goodbye to Rachel, Annie, and Bill. Kris follows suit, then Daniel. Ayden concedes, and with a handshake, a few hugs and kisses on the cheek, fakes disinterest in the fondness he has for them all. 'See ya.'

It's not that he fears looking weak, or less masculine - that's never bothered him. But there has always been something holding him back from 'public displays of affection' - well, just 'displays of affection'. Even in the quiet times together with Daniel, he has been unable to lift a veil which would expose his tangible admiration, respect, and endearment he has for him. For anyone for that matter. He knows that Daniel recognises how he feels, and that has been sufficient for all of their 35 years together, but at times he wishes he were able to be a little more 'overtly' affectionate. Like William is with Annie. *You can't teach old dogs new tricks*, he thinks and smiles.

Daniel and Ayden arrive at Paranga Restaurant more or less at the same time as Kris and Ivan. Ayden, as always, had paid a random stranger to 'help' him reverse his car into a parallel park along the Promenade. He didn't need the 'help' of course, but it makes him smile every time trying to decipher the useless babble of instructions and vague hand signals from the distracted stranger, who is already looking further afield for the next 'client'. Moreover, Ayden adhered to a belief that it is important to give some level of financial support to 'those less fortunate', as his mother would say. God knows, at least they're doing something.

'Is there space?' Daniel inquires, standing at the entrance of the restaurant, but not really actively trying to answer his own question. Ayden walks in and claims an empty table near the front, with a view of the Promenade, removing the 'Reserved' sign and putting it on the bench behind him. An attractive waiter arrives, and Ayden, being already familiar with the wine list, orders a bottle of Waterford Estate cabernet sauvignon. 'And four glasses, of course.' He gets a look from Kris, clearly questioning the expense. 'Well it's a special occasion.' Ayden says. Then turning to Daniel, who is ogling the attractive waiter as he walks away from the table, 'And you... put your tongue in, close your mouth, and wipe the drool off your chin.'

Four glasses are raised, and clink. 'To the fond memories we have,' Daniel says.

'To...' Ayden tries to say her name, but, a little choked, it does not come out, 'her.'

He enjoys spending time with the three of them. With Daniel, of course, it's like wearing a comfortable old (worn out) coat, but he has grown to really love being with Kris and Ivan. The four of them have become great friends through the years, sharing so much in common, and, as the Millennials love to say, 'creating memories' together. They had built up a trust among each other, more than just comradeship, but the warmth of a family none of them individually could boast. They had shared their stories, and were privy to the highs and lows of each other's life. Ayden still remembers first meeting them in Serge's. 'Do you remember that day in Marie's restaurant when we met you?' They all smile.

-§-

'They're there again' Daniel whispers to Ayden, whilst still in the Daimler as they drive by the restaurant enroute to their car park.

'Why are you whispering?' Ayden asks almost incredulously, 'they can't hear you!' He turns into a space on Kloof Street, which 'Christiaan' always kept free for Ayden around this time, knowing he would get some cash, and perhaps some remnants of lunch when they returned.

As they go into the restaurant, they briefly look toward the two guys. They are neatly dressed, one in a well-tailored light green sweater, the other sporting a light linen jacket over a white t-shirt, and both wearing jeans. They are in the same space as always - along the wall near the kitchen, clicking away on their laptops. *Looking so important and busy*, Ayden thinks. *Tossers!*

He and Daniel take their usual spot in the alcove. Marie strides over to them, bottle of Hartenberg cabernet sauvignon, and two glasses in hand, ready to chat.

'So, they're here again?' Daniel says.

'They're here most days.' Marie replies, 'They bought The Lady Hamilton, and are in the middle of major renovations - remodeling the inside completely, all new bathrooms, redoing the floors, repainting the whole place. Lots of work, eh?'

'The Lady Hamilton?' Ayden exclaims. 'Shit, that's huge! What is that, 80 rooms or something?.. renovating?'

'No wonder they look busy.' Daniel says.

Marie nods, 'I know! They plan to reopen in only 5 weeks. Very nice guys. One Dutch, and the other Austrian, no, New Zealand, something! With a weird accent.'

'5 weeks?' Ayden says in disbelief. 'Not possible.'

'Wait a minute,' Daniel interrupts, 'you said they have started renovations? At The Lady Hamilton?'

'Mm,' she hums as she pours two glasses of wine.

'But I can see The Lady Hamilton from the 'sink estate', and there is absolutely no sign of renovations going on... at all!'

'Really?' Marie thinks again. 'Well now I have to find out. Come, I'll introduce you.'

'Not if they own The Lady Hamilton, not in our league, honey!' Ayden declares.

'Is that a black MacBook?' Daniel says, always to the beat of a different drum. 'I haven't seen one like that before.'

Ayden stares at him, 'What?'

'From Hong Kong I believe.' Marie says.

'Ah, fake rip-off then.'

'I don't think you can get fake Apple stuff, can you?'

'Can we get back to The Lady Hamilton? Go and find out...'

Daniel interrupts, 'Shh, one of 'em's coming.'

'Hi, I'm Kris.'

'Hi, nice to meet you. Marie tells us you're renovating The Lady Hamilton?'

'The Lady Hamilton? No, no, The Lady Victoria.'

'Ahhh, Where the fuck is that?'

-§-

There is a bit of laughter, and smiles all 'round. Ivan downs the remnants of his first glass of wine and reaches for the bottle, topping up the others' glass before finishing the bottle on his own. Ayden gets up from the table and heads to the Promenade. 'Gonna have a fag,' he advises his mates.

'I thought you'd given up,' Kris says.

'It's a special occasion!'

It is a beautiful evening. There's a light breeze, not the savage gales that Camps Bay often delivers. Ayden looks across the road, across the bluish, moon-lit sand of the deserted beach and into the dark waters of the Atlantic Ocean. He misses his friend so completely it hurts; part of him is gone. After 'shacking up' with Daniel in London, and the older he grew, the more he allowed people to become significant fixtures in his life. So much so that when they left, had gone, or didn't need him anymore, he was wounded. *Foolish old man,* he thinks to himself. He bums a cigarette from an Afrikaans couple sitting at a table on the footpath, lights up, and wanders across the street, looking back at Paranga. It's a world away from his early life in Northern Ireland.

He is at peace with his life, and who he is now. It certainly was not always easy as a teenager growing up gay in Belfast in the early 80's. A bit like being handed a double whammy. He is not, nor has he ever been, overly analytical about the impact growing up through such civil unrest has had on his adult life. He doesn't consider the number of times he had, necessarily, blocked from his mind the atrocities he had witnessed. For him, and for his friends, it was normal. Normal to regularly have school closed. Normal to have friends one day who were gone the next for whatever reason. Normal to be suspicious of your neighbours, and to keep your thoughts to yourself. Normal to make sure you watch where you are walking and to keep track of where you were. Normal to personally discover an undetonated bomb in a bin next to the garage where he was working part time. *How could any of THAT be normal?*

Of course it wasn't 'doom and gloom' all the time. He did have a great life as a kid in a very secure, stable family. Growing into a young man, he afforded himself the thrill of breaking boundaries. He wasn't rebellious; he and his sister respected their parents too much. But he did feel the need to get out of Belfast, escape to London, and immerse himself in the pleasures of underground clubs when he had the opportunity. Ayden smiles. *What was his name? Ach, didn't matter then, and it certainly doesn't matter now. Good times.*

He draws on his cigarette, enjoying the shot of nicotine in his system again, and the physical action of smoking, and exhales as he turns to look out at the dark, cold water, contemplating why William and Annie always feel the need to pack up their house in Cape Town when they leave. *It's their house!*

-§-

Sauntering into Serge's for lunch on a beautiful summer's day, Daniel and Ayden glance over to Marie who is busy chatting to a very fit looking couple in the opposite alcove, nearest the bar. The young lady is immaculately dressed, although Ayden suspects the attire was intended to look more casual. Marie has her hand resting quite comfortably, a bit too comfortably for Ayden's liking, on the gentleman's broad shoulder. The man looks up at the two of them, Ayden is impressed with the man's physique; impressive arms, highlighted by the thin white t-shirt draped over his shoulders, clinging to his pecs. He has a strong face, the likes of which Ayden has seen before in the boardroom. He imagines he is a businessman of sorts, and that he would be a formidable opponent. Still, there is a gentleness and kindness in his face, which Ayden admires. The man smiles. *Fuck, he's seen me staring.*

'Wow!' exclaims Daniel.

'The view for lunch is improving.' Ayden concurs, and looks at Daniel with a smirk of approval.

Marie waves at them to come over, which Ayden does with great enthusiasm and mock haste. 'You haven't met yet,' Marie states. 'William and Annie, Daniel and Ayden.'

William stands and shakes Ayden's hand, then Daniel's.

'Wow, that's a firm grip.' Ayden says with a wry smile.

'Come and join us, we haven't eaten yet, but we have just opened a bottle of Cederberg sauvignon blanc.' William offers.

'Well, it would be rude not to.' Ayden replies.

Annie nods to them both, somewhat demurely. Marie returns to the table with a small container of ice, ice tongs, and two additional glasses. Annie takes a cube and drops it into her glass of wine.

'So, where are you kids from, and what are you doing here?' Ayden starts, perhaps a little abrasively.

'It's an extremely long and boring story,' Annie says, 'one which I'm sure William will fill you in on... on another occasion. However, in a nutshell, we own a rather beautiful set of properties, of which the main house is around the corner - a tiny hotel - for the discerning traveller,' she adds with a wink.

'How fab.'

'We have a company which oversees the properties remotely, in conjunction with a local manager and staff.' William says.

'We will visit from time to time to ensure standards are maintained, of course.' Annie says, picking up her glass and offering a toast. 'What a delight to meet you both.'

-§-

Ayden remembers very well the first meeting with Annie, but more fondly recalls how different she was in 'real life' after they'd become friends. She was from Dublin, so they had a little in common, but her lineage was quite different to his. She is a petite girl with a strong will. Beautiful, straight blonde hair and classical facial features. To the outside world she would come across as 'proper', exacting and austere, whereas in reality, to all her friends and family, she was loads of fun, devilishly witty, devoutly loyal, and perhaps just a little 'proper'. She boasted many gay friends and, surprisingly, had a vast knowledge of the seedy side of gay culture. She was happy to share her new-found expertise, together with sordid anecdotes, at parties with the right people - always feigning an air of disbelief and scorn. It was truly part of her charm, which drew you in.

William, on the other hand, was a man's man, with no pretense and no time for time wasters. He was a businessman first, but he too was as loyal a friend could be and, perhaps to his detriment, utterly devoted to Annie. Ayden nicknamed him 'Buffalo Bill', given that Annie once sang at a party, 'You can't get a man with a gun', in her best southern accent, to which Ayden declared 'With those 'guns', he's got me.'

He laughs to himself and butts his cigarette on the footpath with his foot, then heads across the street back to Paranga. Still partially reminiscing, he hadn't looked for oncoming traffic, and is dragged back to the present by the screeching tires and sounding horn of a white Audi R8 convertible with personalised plates: FAR Q. Ayden stares for a moment at the car which nearly ran him down. A young white male driver and his 'too-perfect' blonde, female companion, are shouting monosyllabic 'instructions' at him, supported with pseudo-Italianesque hand gestures. He moves aside and motions them forward, gracing them with his best Shakespearean bow. The convertible roars past and the driver lifts his hand, sticking up his middle finger. Ayden is amused, even impressed, that the driver has the mental capacity and dexterity to isolate individual fingers and still be able to continue driving! Years ago, there was a time when he would have lost his temper in a serious manner on such an occasion, and hurled abuse at the driver and his companion, to the embarrassment of everyone within a 50-metre radius. *Too hard*, he thinks.

He settles back into his seat on the terrace.

'That was close.' Kris says, a little concerned. 'We ordered another bottle - it's a special occasion!' He smiles.

Ayden smiles, not wanting to make a fuss, 'Feckin' kids. I tell you what, when I was a boy.'

The waiter returns with the second bottle and puts his hand on Ayden's shoulder. 'Are you OK? Could have been nasty.'

'I'm fine, thanks... better after another glass of wine... just to the top.' Ayden says, tapping the rim of his glass.

The waiter smiles, pours, and leaves.

'Hallmark House, in Maboneng,' Daniel states, looking up from his phone. 'What are you talking about?'

'We were trying to remember where we stayed in Joburg before heading to Kevin Richardson's Lion thingy,' filling Ayden in on the conversation he had missed.

'Ah yes, and they sent us to that massive restaurant for dinner, on the pretense of it being the best food in Maboneng,' Ivan recalls. 'We were the only people there, and the food was just OK.'

'And it was wet and cold…' Ayden adds. 'Not the food, I mean the weather.'

'After the Lion Whisperer, we caught the Rovos Rail back to Cape Town.'

'And saw Kimberly's Big Hole!' Ayden remembers. 'That must have been one of the best trips we did together. A suitcase of clothes for all occasions: both a Lion safari drive, and formal evening wear for the Rovos Rail.'

'We were all struggling with our trousers and our ties, I recall.' Kris smiles.

'Well, it had been a while since I wore a tie.' Ayden says.

~§~

During his years in London, together with Daniel, Ayden had worked a corporate life with his own business, providing all manner of 'satellite', temporary staff for large companies; cleaners, maintenance personnel, secretaries, and other interim office staff. He called it 'Hire Intelligence Staff', and it was an incredibly lucrative business. He enjoyed being the boss, playing that role with aplomb, which necessarily required dressing for the part in Hugo Boss suits and shirts, Armani ties, and Gucci shoes. Ayden relished the business challenge and the busy work, but he also enjoyed the long, boozy lunches, the invites to opening exhibitions and parties, and the afternoon drinks at the pub on a Friday. After the Stockmarket downturn of 2002, with declining business, Ayden managed to sell his company to his business partner, on the promise of guaranteed increased work, for a very handsome sum. It afforded Daniel and him the opportunity to make a new start in South Africa.

It was a complete change of life for them both, and they jumped in with enthusiasm, opening and running the four-bedroom guesthouse, employing and training their own staff, becoming acquainted with the Cape Town 'way of doing things', and enjoying some travel amongst it all.

~§~

The second bottle is finished and Daniel checks his watch. 'Well, we'd better get back to the house.'

'Yeah, us too.' Kris replies. 'Our shout tonight, OK?' There are no objections.

They walk onto the Promenade in the cool night air. It's a lot busier and a lot noisier now, a mix of young locals, black and white, and tourists. The footpath is full with cafe tables and pedestrians. Flashing coloured lights from clubs bounce off the road and off the faces of passers-by.

'Right, lovely to chat.' Ayden says as he turns to walk down the road. 'Come round for a kitchen supper sometime this week. Thursday?' He looks to Daniel for confirmation. 'Thursday!'

Ayden slips a folded ten Rands note into the hand of the random stranger parking 'guard', and they climb into the Daimler. He drives along the Promenade, turns left, and winds up Camps Bay Drive.

His mind can't let her go. He smiles remembering the new restaurant they discovered on Kloof street, and meeting Marie that day she nearly rammed her car into Rachel's on Union Street. Watching it unfold from the prime location in the alcove at Serge's, and being helpless to stop it, like watching a movie. How shaken poor Rachel was as Marie escorted her into the restaurant and served her a cup of tea, Rachel smiling at the two of them but not really seeing them. He remembers when he first chatted with Marie, after Daniel ran after Rachel, fishing for details of her nationality as an ingress to her providing any uncomplicated details of her life, even perhaps a reason for being here, and her being a little elusive. Her 'cock-up' with The Lady Hamilton. Ayden laughs to himself, unaware of Daniel turning his head to stare at him momentarily.

The Daimler heads over the crest between Lion's Head and Table Mountain onto Kloof Nek. He can't count the number of times he's done this drive. *Always such a beautiful view of the city*, Ayden thinks.

Marie and he had become very close friends, and the reality hits him again; he was the only person she chose to confide in. The only person, other than her own brother, who knew why she chose never to return to Europe. He had sworn to secrecy, and not even Daniel knew the real story; for Ayden, a promise is a promise. During those conversations amongst his three friends, as speculation flew about Marie's life, he feigned interest but remained silent.

He had seen only one photo of Lucien, the night Marie, sobbing and unhinged with fear, poured her heart out to him. In the photo, Lucien looked like such a charming, distinguished gentleman. Neat dark hair, grey at the temples, perfect olive skin. The two of them standing tall on Boulevard de la Croisette in Cannes during the Film Festival. He was wearing a natural toned linen suit and a well-pressed white shirt, open to the second button, loafers, and a new Panama hat, complementing, perhaps too perfectly, Marie's wraparound pale olive green summer dress, and diamanté studded heels.

He had received her call the day after the news reports of that terrible business with Oscar Pistorius, and raced around to her apartment. Marie was inconsolable; erratically relaying wild stories of gaslighting and abuse, which took Ayden some time to piece together. She was living in fear once again, believing that one day Lucien would find her. Of course he did! For sure Ayden was more than just a bit suspicious about the 'accident', but he chose not to push for an investigation.

Ayden knew he could never tell his best friends; he couldn't tell anyone! If only half of what Marie was saying was true, how could he put them in the same danger she had lived with all her life, simply by telling them the horrid truth. Better that none of them knew. It was a secret he would take to his grave.

'Ayden... Ayden... AYDEN!' Daniel says with increasing firmness.

He comes back to reality.

'You missed the turn-off. Where the hell are you going? Bloody concentrate.'

Kris

What the fuck am I doing?, he thinks to himself, taking a break from packing a few essential household items in his suitcase and boxes. He finds himself once again on the periphery of his comfortable experiences, but in reality that has never really bothered him, perhaps it even drives him. He looks out of the window of his modern apartment in Friedrichshain, Berlin, at the garden he and Ivan had planted themselves, only a few weeks ago. A garden he doubted he would ever see mature enough to enjoy himself. His apartment building was once a school house in East Berlin. Perfectly symmetrical, but charming, not brutalist. Now developers had sensitively converted it into low rise apartments, and Kris managed to get in early to secure a corner duplex apartment with a garden.

He smiles as he fondles a Korean Buncheong vase ready for packing. He and Ivan had bought a guesthouse in Cape Town on holiday last year, and he had bought the apartment on a holiday some six months earlier. *I need to stop going on holidays*. In the morning they were flying to Cape Town to run a small 7-bedroom guesthouse. *What the fuck am I doing?*, he thinks again.

Everything was, or was going to be, new for Kris - the move to yet another country and continent, his relationship with Ivan, his line of work, driving on the wrong side of the road, and actually driving instead of being chauffeured. He found it cathartic and thrived on change, finding it more invigorating than impeding. For how much longer? He couldn't say, but for now, an exciting new challenge lay ahead.

After a ten-year stint as CEO for a Dutch/Swiss multinational pharmaceutical company in Seoul, South Korea, Kris resigned, but was persuaded to undertake a special assignment throughout Asia by the same company, to be based in Hong Kong. Only a couple of years ago he had met Ivan in Hong Kong and together they had concocted an idea to run a guesthouse, drawing up their first, wine-influenced, business plan on a paper serviette in a crowded bar in Mid-Levels. On holiday together in Cape Town, they found a gorgeous, but significantly ravaged, Victorian homestead, already operating as a b'n'b, and couldn't resist the challenge.

Kris and Ivan have been in Cape Town for four weeks and renovations have just commenced on the tired Lady Victoria bed and breakfast, with a vision of creating a new, fresh, upmarket guesthouse to be called Victoria Boutique Villa. They had decided, rightly or wrongly, to continue employing the staff of the former b'n'b, and mandated the former manager to oversee the movement of builders and tradesmen, with an extremely lucid understanding that nothing goes into or out of the house without the express knowledge and permission of Kris and Ivan. Nothing!

The sun is shining on a beautiful mid-morning in late July and Kris thinks it wise to give a bit of space and efficacious encouragement to their manager, deciding to take a walk for a coffee and croissant with Ivan. 'Take your laptop. We can start working on the new website.' Kris suggests. 'There is that place on Long Street that we have been to before.'

As they meander down Kloof Street, Ivan notices a new cafe/restaurant. 'This looks good. It even has white tablecloths.'

'Great, it's close to the house as well. Let's try it,' Kris says.

They head into the restaurant and choose a table on the side wall next to the kitchen because it has two power outlets. A very well-spoken girl takes their order - a cappuccino and croissant, and a simple black coffee - no extra hot water. They busy themselves with details on their website, sipping coffee, and from time to time Kris looks up, breathing in his surroundings and reaffirming his delight in being here in this city. He watches as an attractive, tall lady, with tied up dark hair, wearing a comfortable but stylish patterned dress, low heels, and vibrant red lipstick, walks in and heads to the kitchen. *The owner?* he guesses.

Coming out of the kitchen, she approaches their table, the light breeze catching her dress, which exposes her long legs, 'Anything more I can get for you gentlemen?'

'Not at the moment,' Kris says, looking up at her, 'We love your restaurant. I'm guessing you're the owner.'

'Oui.'

 Immediately detecting no pretense in her French, 'Hi, I'm Kris.'

'Marie.' She extends her hand and they shake. 'Hmm, I'm guessing either Belgian or Nederlander.'

Kris smiles. Clearly she speaks Dutch as well. 'Dutch, correct - Limburg, Maastricht. At least you didn't say German!' He jokes, believing the joke would not go to waste. He continues, already knowing the answer, 'And I'm guessing, France or southern Belgium.'

'France, yes, from Lille... years ago now.'

'Ah, we were practically neighbours,' Kris replies, sensing, with her statement there is more to the story, but it was clearly off-limits... for now.

Ivan jumps in to introduce himself, awkwardly trying a similar joke related to his nationality, perhaps not realising it would be lost on Europeans.

'Are you guys travelling, on holiday?' Marie asks.

'We bought a guesthouse last year on holiday here…' Kris says.

'As you do.' Marie interjects, jesting.

'It was called 'The Lady Victoria', it's in Gardens, just a short walk from here.' Kris notices that Marie is distracted by one of her staff, absorbing only bits of his story. 'After we bought it, we both had to go back to Hong Kong and Berlin to finish up some business. Now we're back and have started renovations…' He continues talking, but knows that Marie is not listening. He could have said anything but sticks to his story. 'So we need to get out of the house regularly to get the dust and disasters out of our heads.'

Marie returns her attention to them both, taking an interest in what Ivan has to say, and comments appropriately. As she talks, Kris can't help being intrigued by Marie's distracted gaze past her staff and across the street. What an interesting character.

Marie, concluding her story, 'Well you have a lot of people to meet. Guesthouse owners are coming out of our ears in this town. I think the looming World Cup has drawn them out of the woodwork. All lovely people - well, the people I know at least. And that's all that matters. I'll introduce you to them all.'

Kris smiles. 'Sounds good.' Still sensing a degree of melancholy and circumspection in Marie's demeanor, he is drawn to her as a friend with a warm sense of compassion and European familiarity.

'Now, let's have a look at the wine list for lunch.' Ivan concludes.

The renovations are complete: Victoria Boutique Villa, Cape Town's newest guesthouse, is open for business. Time for a party! Kris charges their manager with the task of inviting fellow guesthouse owners, Marie and her brother Pierre, and of course, it's always a good idea to invite the neighbours.

There are sufficient people to make the gathering interesting, not too many nor too few, and Kris does his best to get around to meet everyone. Secretly, however, he is on a mission tonight to spend some time chatting with Marie, to get to know her a bit more. He knows there's more to her than the simple facade of 'restaurateur from France' that she presents. After he meets Rachel from Freedom House in the living room, and subsequently introduces her to Ivan, Kris seeks out Marie. He finds her in the kitchen with the staff, helping them make some canapés.

'You're supposed to be enjoying the party,' Kris says, 'not working.'

'You will find out that when there's food involved, I can't help myself,' Marie replies.

'Come out to the veranda. Table Mountain is lit up tonight, and you get quite a nice view from the side of the house. Have you got a drink?'

Kris leads the way, and Marie follows, picking up her glass from the kitchen bench. Marie nods politely to a number of people enroute to the veranda. *She knows everybody*, Kris thinks. It is a cool evening, and there is no wind, making it very pleasant to be outside.

'That's a beautiful dress.' Kris compliments Marie. 'I doubt you got that here.'

Marie smiles. 'Indeed, a remnant from Paris.' She confides.

'Pierre is not here tonight?'

'No, sorry, he is busy with a friend, so I'm told.'

'Got a better offer then.'

'His loss, certainly not yours or your guests'. Let's say he's not one for always making the best choices. Maybe it runs in the family.' She laughs to emphasise the joke.

Kris smiles. The invitation for digging further is there, but he thinks it's too easy. 'How long have you been in Cape Town?'

'A few years already, I guess. I have sort of lost count.'

'... and in the restaurant?'

'Not that long, maybe just over a year. But tell me...' she adds without missing a beat, 'you and Ivan, you must have been travelling all over the world?'

Kris smiles, not from the question, but from her cunning reversal of interrogation. 'I have lived and worked in three continents, and far more cities...' He looks at her, winks, then takes a swig of champagne.

'So why Cape Town?'

'Ah, a question for us each to answer.'

'You first.' She smiles.

'In a nutshell... why not? It is a naturally beautiful city: the sea, the mountain, some of the best wine and food in the world. I think we can enjoy an extremely exceptional quality of life here.'

'You see...' she says, 'Exactly what I was going to say.' Marie smiles and takes a sip.

'I mean, for us, we were looking for a change of life and a change in the pace of life. Finished in corporate, and jumped into hospitality. So what brought you to Cape Town?' Kris ramps up to level two of his inquisition, only to have his mission derailed by Ivan waltzing into the scene with Rachel on his arm.

'Rachel, can I introduce you to Marie?' Ivan says.

Kris watches Marie swing around, and from the corner of her eye she sees him and smiles. He smiles, defeated.

'Marie!' Rachel says with surprise. 'We know each other. It's a village here.'

Walking back into the living room, Kris decides to leave it at that. Marie knew too well his plan, and was too defensive to allow him into her world at this stage. That's not to say he hadn't tried other angles, including Pierre, which was quite fruitless. *Why is he not at the party? Did we really upset him? He is a weird guy.*

-§-

Kris and Ivan had made Serge's their 'second home', particularly as the renovations continued, but even as that drew to a close and they prepared for opening, they frequented Marie's restaurant almost daily. A few weeks before the opening of Victoria Boutique Villa, Kris and Ivan step into Serge's on a beautiful afternoon for a bite to eat and a glass of wine. Looking for Marie, they discover she is not in this afternoon. Heading to their 'new' favourite spot: the alcove closest to the bar, and before they are seated or settled, they are accosted by a tall gentleman with dark, wavy hair. He is wearing uncomfortable looking trousers and a slightly untucked, slightly off-white shirt, and almost raced to their table from behind the bar. Without taking a breath, he brashly introduces himself, 'Hi, I'm Pierre. I'm Marie's brother.' In a state of disbelief, worthy of his over-enthusiastic, bombastic introduction, Kris and Ivan helplessly stare at him. There is a silence between the three of them which you can almost see, like a fog, as he waits for a suitable response... for any response.

'Umm, OK, nice to meet you, umm, perhaps we can see the menu, please?' Kris initiates.

'Oh yeah, umm, yes, of course, sure, of course.' Pierre walks briskly to the lectern of the maître d' and returns with a menu.

'Perhaps you have another one for Ivan?'

'Oh yeah.' he laughs to himself, a little embarrassed and confused. He runs off and returns with another menu. He hands it to Ivan and stands at the table waiting - staring.

Despite knowing what he wants, Kris ponders the menu, hoping to get a little reprieve from the vigilant, yet vacant, eye of their invasive waiter.

Kris finally starts to suggest 'Give us a minu…'

'I'm Marie's brother.' Pierre interrupts. 'Oh, I think I told you that.' He looks out into the street. 'Marie is not here this afternoon.'

'Yes, OK, so we can see.' Ivan confirms.

Thinking this might be a chance to learn more about Marie, Kris begins his interrogation. 'Did you leave Europe together with Marie?'

Not hearing the question, Pierre announces, 'I have a cat now….' Silence. 'Would you like to see a picture of my cat?' Silence… then without receiving confirmation, he produces a photo from the back pocket of his trousers, of a cat, which is being held by a well-tanned and toned, shirtless man… silence. 'What do you think?'

Both Ivan and Kris realise the presentation of the photo and the fatuous question, coupled with the extended delay in additional comment, was an invitation to a conversation relating more to the bare-chested man, over the actual cat. An invitation they both ignore.

'Nice cat.' Kris declares. 'I'll take the chopped salad with beef and a glass of sauvignon blanc.'

'I'll have the same.' Ivan follows, handing back the photo and the menu.

Pierre brings out their meals and, for an unknown reason, stays by their table, thinking it important to keep his customers company, watching them eat.

'When will Marie be in?' Ivan inquires.

'Hmm, shortly I believe. I have to get home because my friend is looking after my cat.'

Realising his interrogation down this route is a completely lost cause, Kris replies 'OK. Great. We'll see you another time, I'm sure.' Silence. 'Can you get the bill for us?' Silence!

-§-

A few months after the opening of their guesthouse, Marie introduces them both to William and Annie at Serge's. Just a normal lunch by all accounts, he and Ivan having the usual chopped salad with beef and a glass of sauvignon blanc, when, as a younger looking couple walk briskly down Kloof street, Marie jumps out from behind the bar, runs out of the restaurant and returns together with the couple, all three standing on the footpath. 'Ivan and Kris, may I introduce you to Annie and William.' Marie says, task completed, she heads back to the bar.

'Hi, I'm Kris and this is Ivan, just to clear that up,' Kris says with a smile, extending his hand and standing to formally meet them both. 'I dare say it's somewhat easier working out who is who with the two of you,' he adds.

Ivan takes to Annie like a moth to a flame, and as Kris chats to William he is increasingly taken by his clear business mind, perhaps even a bit hopeful that he can converse with someone again on a similar level to that which he was accustomed in Korea.

'We established a company here, and registered it with the CIPC, to oversee all the admin of the properties,' William says. 'We have a few interesting ventures, but we're always on the lookout for exciting new projects. Currently we are negotiating the purchase of a slightly run-down game reserve in the north, near the border with Botswana. We think it will be a good investment and once it's all 'fixed up', I think we can attract a different level of tourist.'

'It would be good to chat with you about your company and setting it up in South Africa a bit more, if we have an opportunity.' Kris says with a genuine interest in the operation.

Annie interrupts her chat with Ivan, realising the time, after looking at her delicate Blancpain watch. 'We really must keep moving, Bill.' Annie says. 'So sorry to have to rush off. We have an appointment at the hotel.' She slides her arm around the back of William's impressive, well-developed torso and pulls him into her. 'But listen, why don't the two of you swing by the house sometime and we can open a bottle and get to know you some more. We have the boutique hotel on Upper Union Street. Pop in there and they can direct you to the house. We will let them know. It's Ivan and…'

'Kris' Kris says filling in the gap.

'Perfect.' Annie confirms.

'Better still,' William adds, 'If you're free Sunday, why not come over for a braai. We'll get some others over as well. Perhaps Ayden and Daniel are free. Do you know them?'

'Yes, we have met. Sounds like a plan.' Kris says,

William rushes inside the restaurant to scribble details down on a piece of paper. Kris watches him smile at Marie behind the bar. *Is she blushing?*

He returns, handing the note to Kris. 'Say around 1pm?'

'Perfect.'

'Please don't bring anything,' Annie says, 'We have plenty.' She turns to William, 'We have to go, BB.' Turning to head down the street, 'See you on Sunday.'

Kris looks at Ivan, who is clearly a little awed by the encounter.

'He's a fit bunny.' Ivan says.

William's good looks and fit form certainly hadn't gone unnoticed by Kris, but he is never one to make a comment. 'Nice couple,' he simply adds. 'What do you think 'BB' stands for?'

'Big Bucks?' Ivan suggests, with a big smile.

'Well, you two are rather lucky,' Marie says as she returns to their table, 'Not many people get an invite to the house for a braai on their first introduction. He's good-looking, isn't he?'

Kris watches both Marie and Ivan stare out into the street, with smiles on their faces. He smiles and takes a sip of wine.

-§-

It had been on his mind for many years, and now seemed like the perfect time, place, and opportunity to give it a go. Once the country had begun to get back to normal, a few months after Nelson Mandela died, Kris found a property for rent in the city. 'Perfect,' he says.

He signs the papers at the property with a very happy, overdressed realtor looking over his shoulder to ensure nothing is left unsigned or initialised. 'Divine,' she exclaims in her thick Afrikaans accent. She collects the document, shoves it in her fake Gucci handbag, hands Kris the keys and shakes his hand before walking out, awkwardly negotiating the steps into the paved pedestrian mall in her ridiculous stilettos. Kris amuses himself watching her struggle out of the door. He turns back for a moment to look at the space and smiles, the Jan Royce Gallery will finally become a reality.

In the next few months Kris launches himself into an exhaustive private campaign to discover new young artists, and to acquaint himself with the established artist elite of South Africa. He finds it an exhilarating process, and like everything with which he has challenged himself over the years, he immerses himself into the journey 'boots and all'.

Exhibitions come and go, and Jan Royce Gallery becomes a 'go-to' for international visitors, locals, and expats who are serious about collecting contemporary art by South Africans. Kris has a keen, critical eye for good art; he is not interested in presenting the African wild animals or Zulu beads and colours that the tourists expect, and he knows his clients appreciate his penchant for well-crafted pieces. He finds himself shipping pieces all over the world, or hand-delivering them to outrageously massive homes perched high on the cliffs of Cape Town's coastal suburbs.

Kris looks up from his laptop this sunny afternoon to greet the tall, well-dressed man walking into the gallery, clearly interested in the Stanislaw Trzebinski bust in the centre of the showroom. He is holding a well-worn Panama hat in his left hand and is removing his classic RayBans with his right.

'It's a beautiful piece.' Kris says to open the dialogue.

'Oui, it certainly is.' The gentleman replies, with a strong French accent. 'Is it by a South African artist?'

'Yes, Stanislaw Trzebinski. Kenyan born, but now is working and living as an artist in Cape Town.'

'Magnificent work, amazing detail.'

'I agree, Trzebinski has an eye for detail, sculpting an incredibly lifelike image. Then he enjoys 'playing' with the figure with fragments of coral or the like, stemming from his love of the ocean.'

'Aha. Bronze?'

'Yes, bronze, one of seven. Cast here in a foundry in Woodside. It's called 'Encrusted'.'

'I'm looking for a new piece for my apartment in Paris to celebrate… well, you know, new beginnings. Getting rid of deadwood and starting afresh.' He picks up the weighty bronze, lifting it with considerable ease.

Nervously, Kris helps him put the bust back on the plinth. 'Can I show you other works by the same artist perhaps?'

'Mmm, what else do you have, perhaps something a little smaller; I need to get it back on a plane. This one on your desk? Very intriguing. By the same artist, I'm assuming, with the use of coral.'

'Yes, correct. The coral creating a type of bust. Also a bronze, but this one is a unique piece. I was actually wanting to keep this one for my private collection.'

The gentleman smiles callously, 'Well, I'm afraid I'm going to have to take this from you. I'll have this one.'

'I'll be sad to see it go.'

'I should be able to get it on a plane, right? You know, business class.'

'I'm sure you can. It's not too heavy. In hold or cabin?'

'Cabin should be fine, right? It's not big.'

'I can wrap it appropriately and sort out all the paperwork, including an authentication certificate, and an invoice for customs in France. It will be ready for you later this afternoon.'

'Fantastic. Shall I pay for it now? Is cash OK?'

'Mmm, sure, cash is king!'

Kris swaggers into the house holding a bottle of Moët. Ivan, from the kitchen, recognises the grin. 'Congratulations?' He asks.

'Sold one of Stas's pieces to a French guy this afternoon. Better still, no delivery! He took it with him, and was going to take it back to Paris as cabin baggage, business class. Perfect!'

'Well done, you. Which piece?'

'My favorite; the coral bust.'

'Oh no, such a nice piece.' Getting two flutes from the cupboard.

'Good looking guy; strong too. Nice clothes, clearly tailored, and expensive shoes. Determined face, dark hair, a bit grey around the sides, and amazing olive skin. He looks after himself for sure.'

'Is he 'family'?' Ivan inquires with a wink.

'Don't think so. For sure we would never become friends. I didn't care for his arrogant manner.' He pops the cork of the Moët. 'He said he was celebrating a new life. I got an uneasy feeling about him, but he bought some art.' Kris pours two glasses of champagne, and he and Ivan toast.

A few years later it was decided at a kitchen supper at the guesthouse of Daniel and Ayden, that the four of them would take a trip to see a special lion reserve north of Pretoria, followed by the uber-luxurious Rovos Rail trek back to Cape Town. Now, as he stands on the railway station platform waiting for the famed train to arrive, Kris is hoping that the second part of their dual experience holiday is better than the first part. The luxury tent accommodation was fine, and waking up to see wildebeest only twenty meters from his tent was both exhilarating and unnerving. The day drives were good, and watching their host, the owner of the reserve, walk with the lions was incredible, if not a little concerning. But Kris couldn't reconcile the rhetoric of the owner versus the reserve set-up: saving the lions from being raised in captivity for big game hunters, only to put them in captivity. In addition, four days was way too long.

It was Ayden's idea to go to the lion reserve, and Kris liked his decisive manner and follow-through. He assumed it stemmed from his business days in London. He is a good-looking guy, Kris has always thought, for his age. He would have been a stunner in his youth. A strong, almost stern face, piercing eyes, and now, just remnants of dark brown hair. He is not portly, as you might expect, but kept himself in shape, perhaps mostly through work and a busy routine. He isn't tall, but well-proportioned, he has a big chest, large shoulders, and very large feet. Kris smiles remembering the first time he noticed Ayden's feet, watching him get out of the Daimler on one occasion wearing fantastic Gucci loafers, clearly a surviving artefact of a life of excess in London.

The train arrives, and passengers are individually called to board, averting a crass clambering of impatient, or self-assured, important people - the nouveau riche - pushing their way on board first. Kris and Ivan get into their cabin and Kris smiles. *Now, this is more like it.* The porter delivers their luggage, Ivan asks for some whisky, and Kris arranges to have some shirts ironed in preparation for dinner later that night. As the train eases away from the station, Kris makes his way to the lounge car and settles in with a glass of wine and a book. Smiling to himself as he remembers his Sundays at the Seoul Grand Hyatt and afternoons in the Blue Bar in the Hong Kong Four Seasons.

In the dining car for the second seating of dinner, a table is set for just the four of them. Kris walks into the car adjusting his tie, which he has not worn in a long time. To his amusement, Ayden and Daniel, already seated at the table, are likewise struggling with the tight band of silk wrapped around their neck. 'Good evening. Ivan will be here shortly,' Kris advises, 'He's trying to remember how to do a half-Windsor, or some Italian knot he learned in Australia. I left him to it.'

'This is something else, eh?' Ayden says with clear delight.

'Certainly beats waking up in a tent next to a herd of wildebeest.'

'Confusion.' Daniel states, whilst buttering his bread roll with a polished silver knife.

'About what?' Ayden jumps in before Kris has a chance, with his usual level of annoyance.

'It's not a herd of wildebeest, it's a confusion of wildebeest.'

'They didn't look confused to me,' Kris says, 'That's why I quietly zipped up the tent and went back to bed.'

Ivan walks in, still struggling with his collar. 'Once upon a time in a land far, far away, I was able to do this up.'

'Oh sit down and stop making a scene.' Ayden says with a smile. 'At least you can do your pants up.'

'Way too much information, my friend.' Ivan sits in the chair next to the window and looks out admiring the vast, majestic landscape slowly passing by.

'We've ordered a bottle of white to start,' Ayden says.

'I'm not sure anything can go down my throat with this shirt buttoned up so tightly around my neck,' Daniel replies.

Ivan looks away from the window, 'Ask for a straw,' grabbing his serviette from the table and resting it on his knee.

'I don't think you'll have any trouble getting things down your throat. You never have before, so why start now,' Ayden says with a smirk.

'Again… too much information,' Ivan replies.

Kris smiles and squeezes Ivan's knee under the table. He has been able to enjoy the good things in life, but nothing can replace spending time with good friends, wherever that is. He would never lay bare his inner thoughts or feelings to his friends, but somehow he knows they feel the same; nothing needs to be stated, nothing needs to be verbalised or made clear. It is an unspoken understanding amongst good friends.

Rachel

She is so elated, it's the best news of her life. She almost expects bluebirds to come and sit on her shoulder and chirp cheerfully, and bunnies and other furry forest animals to gather 'round waiting for her to sing - like Snow White in the Disney animation. The afternoon sun is smiling down on her as she walks out of the Mediclinic Hospital main entrance and heads toward the car park. She stops and takes a deep breath. *Thank God*. The cancer was officially in remission, the chemo could stop, her hair would grow back - no more wigs. She felt on top of the world. She had always nurtured, unconceitedly, a delight in being a positive soul, but over the past year it had not always been easy to play that role. Now, feeling invincible in her own quirky way, and becoming as deliriously joyful as a young girl on Christmas morning, with a mixture of excitement and relief, she couldn't work out what to do next, or where to go, or whom to tell. In reality, she had very few really close friends in Cape Town to tell. Her staff at the guesthouse didn't need to know. The three or four acquaintances she had met when buying the guesthouse were probably not available - too busy. Her friends in the UK? *It's a bit hard to share a glass of champagne with them when I'm here,* she thinks, and smiles. 'Let's just get on with the day, and see how it unfolds,' she buoyantly mutters to herself as she heads toward her car.

Rachel had purchased the pale grey Datsun Sunny B210 when she first arrived in Cape Town. It was in good condition for an old secondhand car, and it cost next to nothing. In all the years she has driven it through the streets of Cape Town - to the gym, to the shops, to the theatre - it has never given her any trouble or cost her more than the fuel and some oil. She didn't 'love' it, but it did the job.

I'll pick up some things at Checkers for the guesthouse, she thinks to herself as she pulls out of the hospital car park and right onto Hutt Street. She crosses Camp Street and turns left onto Union. 'Now... the car park, or park on the street?' Dialoguing herself. Slowing down slightly, she looks to her right into the car park behind Checkers... *looks fu...uull*, she sings in her head, embellishing the final strains of the thought, as if she were in a musical. She turns her attention forward, and astonished, looks directly into the face of an attractive woman in a black car driving straight toward her on the wrong side of the road. Rachel slams on her brakes. The two cars stop within centimetres of each other. 'Oh my word, that was close. Another Continental, I'm guessing... or an American...' She looks intensely again through her dirty windscreen at the woman. 'No, European for sure.' Rachel decides to reverse a little, and steer into the car park behind Checkers.

She finds a park, and, not giving the incident any further thought, strides up the stairs back onto Union street and is nearly knocked flying by a frantic woman apologising profusely.

'I'm so sorry,' she says frantically. 'My head was elsewhere, too many years of driving in France.'

'That's fine - that was almost twice, bumping into each other,' chirps Rachel. 'Are you OK?'

'I'm fine. It could have been a lot worse. Just as well I'm a slow driver,' she says, and not being able to help herself, giggles, clearly still a bit in shock.

'I'm so sorry.'

'It's fine, really. It got my heart racing again....good for the immune system.'

'Listen, I own the restaurant across the street. Let me get you a coffee, or tea, or something stronger. I insist.'

'Well, who can say no to a nice cup of tea?' *I'd rather a glass of bubbles,* she thinks. 'I'm Rachel.'

'Marie.'

Marie leads her into the restaurant and Rachel has a quick look around, noticing the two handsome gents in the front alcove, both dressed to look casual, but smart and clearly with due attention to detail. She had not been here before. It's a nice looking place, simple, clean, almost new, she suspects. There is room for at least a dozen tables, all with beautiful crisp white tablecloths, a small bar to the right, and a beautiful old style open fireplace at the back. She asks for a cup of English Breakfast tea, but insists a

Twinings tea bag would be sufficient - never wanting to make a fuss. 'Milk but no sugar, please.' Marie rushes off and returns very quickly with the tea and a small cup of coffee. Quaint, so European. They chat for a short time - long enough for Rachel to feel warmly connected to Marie, and they agree to catch up again. Rachel adds her promise to come back to the restaurant. As she leaves, she instinctively gives Marie a kiss on both cheeks, then hands her a business card with her contact details and heads out the door, nodding to the handsome gents on her way out. She skips across Kloof, then Union, no sooner having crossed the street than one of the men from the restaurant runs up behind her and calls out to her.

'Excuse me, pardon me.'

Rachel spins around. 'Oh, hello, did I leave something behind? Did I drop something on the street? I must be more careful.'

'No, no. Sorry to startle you. I'm just in Serge's and couldn't help overhear your conversation with the owner. You mentioned that you're from the UK and that you have a guesthouse.'

'Oh, yes.'

'Sorry, I'm Daniel.'

'No need to be sorry,' she jests, which is met with a curious look, and silence. 'Hi Daniel, I'm Rachel. Yes, I have Freedom House, on De Lorentz Street.'

'OK, well we have literally just started business at our guesthouse in Oranjezicht, Montrose Manor. It would be great, if it's OK with you, to catch up one day and, you know, compare notes, so to say. Perhaps we could arrange to have lunch one day at Serge's.' Whilst talking, Daniel is fossicking in his rather large 'man-bag'. He finds a business card. 'Here are our contact details,' handing her a fresh business card, 'literally 'straight off the press'.' He smiles proudly.

Rachel studies the card, 'Ayden and Daniel. Are you a couple?'

'For lack of a better term, yes, we are.'

Rachel's heart sinks. *More gay guys!* 'That would be absolutely splendid,' she says. 'Wonderful to meet you, and I look forward to meeting again and being introduced to your man.' She smiles and they each head their own way in opposite directions.

Rachel continues enroute toward Checkers, almost skipping, and with a huge smile on her face, having met two new people in the space of just an hour. That's why she loves Cape Town. As she sails into the entrance, she bumps into a tall, olive-skinned man with neat dark, wavy hair, greying at the temples, dressed in a lightweight, well-tailored dark suit and an open-neck chambray shirt. She smells his expensive, cedar-wood cologne. 'Oh sorry, sorry. Not concentrating.'

'Excusez-moi, pardon me,' he says, grabbing Rachel by her upper arms in a firm grip to stop her from falling. Rachel enjoys, for a moment, the comforting strength of the man's hands holding her. It's been such a long time since she has been held by a man. In a stupidly romantic manner, she looks up to find his eyes, but he releases her, and continues walking, as if on a mission.

M mmm, dishy! Rachel thinks. *Should I try for a hat-trick? No, he's bound to be gay too! Or a spy!* She laughs to herself and walks into the supermarket.

Driving back to Freedom House, she turns into a park on De Lorentz in front of the guesthouse. She sits in her car for a few minutes, reflecting on the day so far. No more cancer, two new friends, and bumping into a handsome stranger. *Things could be worse.*

Rachel met with Daniel and Ayden for lunch or a tea in Serge's on many occasions over several weeks. She was enjoying their developing friendship, and the connection with the UK. Despite quite a different approach to the hospitality business, she enjoys comparing notes on their respective guesthouses: bookings for the season, where to get the best OJ and bacon for breakfast. Moreover she just enjoys spending time with them both.

Marie is not in Serge's this afternoon, when the three of them are enjoying a light lunch and a bottle of JC le Roux sparkling wine, on Rachel's recommendation. It is the first time that Rachel met Marie's brother, Pierre, who is attempting service once again. Ayden seemed rather annoyed by the persistent presence of Pierre, and the lull in conversation is testament to his annoyance. It's almost like watching a Geiger counter in reverse: Every time Pierre comes near, Ayden talks less, and when Pierre is afar, Ayden talks incessantly. She amuses herself with the analogy, wanting to move Pierre, like a pawn, in various locations around the room to see the effect it has on Ayden. To be fair to Ayden, Pierre seems unable to read social situations, incapable of recognising that he is not part of the conversation, nor is he invited to be part. In fact, as harsh as it seemed to Rachel, he is simply a waiter, and he should get on with his job! He is quintessentially socially awkward.

Rachel takes another swig of her bubbles, at the same time the three of them notice a grey Jeep heading in the direction of the city. It slows down at Serge's, the male passenger looks into the restaurant, which is quite empty, he relays something to the driver, then it speeds off in the same direction. 'That was weird,' Rachel says.

'That happens all the time with that car.' Pierre says, who had silently moved into a position right behind them at their table. Ayden, Daniel, and Rachel slowly turn to look at him in disbelief.

After coffee, the two gents excuse themselves, returning to their guesthouse in order to relieve their staff. Rachel admires their 'hands-on' approach, and from what she had ascertained during lunch, their exacting control over their staff to maintain the standards they wanted for their guests. It's not her method, for sure.

Rachel sat on her own in Serge's for another 15-20 minutes after Ayden and Daniel had left, sipping on another glass of bubbles, which Pierre had offered on the house. She absolutely adored meeting new people, and it seemed that Cape Town was a city that enabled it - more than in the UK; perhaps the spirit of the city even encouraged it. *Or perhaps expats everywhere just make an effort to meet new people*, she mused.

She remembers fondly the occasion of meeting William and Annie about a year ago, at Manna Epicure, just a short walk further up Kloof Street toward the mountain. She had been introduced informally by the people from whom she had bought Freedom House, and the three of them met for a coffee. Rachel thinks William is an extremely attractive and well-built man; rugged good looks and a kick-ass smile, and is both witty and charming. Annie, on the other hand, takes a bit of warming to. She looks like a model, as far as Rachel's concerned: amazingly proportioned, beautiful straight blonde hair that seems to just enjoy being tossed gently by the breeze. She has a beautiful, smiley face with dreamy eyes that can look sad sometimes. Her cheeks are well-defined and her lips, although thin, are so magnificently made up. She is thinner than Rachel, but fit looking. Not tall, but Rachel imagined she could hold her own in a fight if she needed to. A character for sure, and a force to be reckoned with. It was while Rachel was taking another bite of her carrot cake that Annie made the remark about a large, bombastic woman walking into the cafe, 'you don't want to knock her beer over at a party'. Rachel later started believing that it was Annie's subconscious idiocentric warning. William and Annie in many respects were like chalk and cheese, yet inseparable, deeply in love, and indisputably perfect for each other. She thoroughly enjoyed their company as a couple, but would never think of asking Annie to join her for a cup of tea and a chin-wag. Rachel just didn't have the confidence.

About a month later, Rachel receives an invitation to the opening of another guesthouse just around the corner from Freedom House. *The city is becoming overrun with accommodation*, she thinks. Not one to miss a good party and to meet new people, she sends her acceptance via email to the manager of the Victoria Boutique Villa.

It's a cool evening, clear and no wind - a definite bonus for this time of year. Rachel walked from her tiny apartment to the guesthouse, heading straight up Bath Street and right onto Kelvin Street. Victoria Boutique Villa was there on the corner, not hard to miss, lit up like a Christmas tree. She introduced herself to the door attendant, a very striking, tall, young black guy, and was admitted into the garden. She grabbed a glass of bubbles and looked for the two owners, whom she knew only by name, Kris and Ivan. The early 1900s Victorian homestead looks magnificent. It was beautifully renovated, maintaining many original features - the cast iron lace along the wrap-around veranda, ornate moulded-tin ceilings, and hand-painted lead-light windows - and now updated with contemporary fittings, art, and furniture.

Rachel stares at various details of the ceiling in the living room, slowly spinning on the spot, in a bit of a daze. She looks past the ceiling rose, following the line of the ornate cornice and down to the fireplace mantle then notices an attractive man wearing dark jeans, an open-neck pale blue shirt, and a well-tailored burnished black jacket, approaching her, 'What do you think?' he says as he stretches out his arms.

Rachel, not wanting to be too funny nor give the wrong impression on her first meeting, decides not to comment on his looks and fabulous dress sense in response to his question. 'The house? It is very beautiful.'

'Hi, I'm Kris, one of the owners.'

'Ohh, I was just looking to meet you. Hi, I'm Rachel. I own Freedom House, which is practically around the corner.'

'Ah, OK, I see, nice to meet you. There are a number of guesthouses in this area - must be the right suburb to be in, right? I still don't know if we are in Gardens or Tamboerskloof. Anyway, welcome and, again, great to meet you.' He holds up his glass, inviting Rachel to join him in a toast, their glasses clink. 'Proost, cheers... I'll see if I can find Ivan so you can meet him as well.' Kris turns and heads out of the room, and returns a moment later with another well-dressed man; dark jeans, a crisp white shirt, and a light brown linen jacket. He is sporting dark-rimmed glasses, and his hair is greying. He has a kind, open face with sparkling green eyes. He is about her height, not muscular, but certainly manly. 'Rachel, this is Ivan.' A short introduction and Kris excuses himself to mingle with other guests.

Ivan and Rachel chat for a while, learning a bit about each other through mostly peripheral details - where they were before Cape Town, how long they'd been here, what nationality they were - all the time both of them accepting a top-up of champagne. They also discover their mutual enjoyment of theatre, at which Rachel is overjoyed. 'Well, at last I have a theatre buddy,' she declares. They clink their glasses to that.

'Listen,' Ivan jumps in, 'there is a production of 'Chess' playing at a small theatre in Camps Bay.'

'Theatre on the Bay.' Rachel assists.

'Yeah, that's it. It's on next week. I'm very curious to see how they do it in such a small venue, with very little space for a large set, and a big company, I'm guessing, and where do you put the musicians? I mean the score is huge. Would you like to come with me? Kris is not one for musicals.'

Rachel is a little overwhelmed by the information, to which she had never given any thought before, least of all about a show she knows nothing about, 'That sounds wonderful. I don't know it at all.'

'One of my favourites. I think the music is wonderful. Book by Tim Rice and the music and lyrics by Benny and Björn - you know - the boys from ABBA.' *My gosh, he knows so much about this stuff!* 'It's a date. How exciting, we're off to see a musical together already.'

Ivan smiles warmly at Rachel, gestures to the staff for another top-up, and invites her to come and meet some other guests on the veranda.

There are only a handful of people at the party, some fellow guesthouse owners; some she knows, some not, and she notes the neighbours were wisely invited. An interesting collection of people, and to some extent, an impressive crowd, given that Kris and Ivan have only been here for a few months.

'Rachel, can I introduce you to Marie.' Ivan says, as Marie, wearing a beautiful, sexy black number, and matching heels, swings her head around, allowing her long dark hair to follow freely a second later.

'Marie!' Rachel says with surprise. 'We know each other. It's a village here,' she says to Ivan, Immediately feeling dowdy in her dull outfit, as she looks Marie up and down in a casually envious manner.

'Then I don't need to tell you that Marie owns one of the best restaurants in Cape Town.' Ivan declares. 'But Marie, darling, and this may be the champagne talking, you have to do something with Pierre! He is no asset to your restaurant. We are in the habit now of driving by to see if he is there before we decide whether to come in.'

'Oh my word, that was you the other day, in the Jeep,' Rachel says, piecing it together.

'Could well have been.'

Marie smiles reservedly. 'In due course.'

Rachel detects something more in her comment, but accepts it at face value, still wishing she had worn something different.

'Who's for a top-up?' Ivan looks curiously into the street, then pivots dramatically, and heads toward the house to find someone with the champagne.

The staff and guests have left, save for Rachel and Marie, who remain chatting on the veranda with Kris and Ivan. Kris opens one last bottle of Bollinger, with an admirable theatricality. 'I don't pop my cork for every guy I see,' he sings. They all laugh drunkenly.

'Why didn't Daniel and Ayden come tonight?' Rachel asks.

'Ah... let's blame that on our esteemed manager, who fucked up that invitation like a...'

Rachel watches Ivan in his drunken state as he, rather unsuccessfully, searches for an appropriate and suitably witty analogy.

'... like a bull in a china shop.' Ivan roars laughing, to the bemused smiles of his friends. Rachel can't figure it out at all. *Too much to drink!*

'We regret that we messed that up.' Kris adds.

'C'est la vie,' Marie reassures. 'There will be plenty more opportunities for us to all get drunk together in this town.'

In the morning, Rachel wakes up with quite the hangover. It's been a long time since she's been down this road. The last time she remembers feeling like this was after she had sold the tea room in Brighton. It was only a few weeks after her husband died, and with the sale of the house and the tea room, she felt a need to celebrate in a serious way for once!

When she opened the shop, it was deliriously exciting. She really enjoyed owning and running The Little Tea Room just off Kingsway. She thought it would give her the chance to meet new people, or at least get out of the house and do something for herself, but it achieved only one of those goals: getting out of the house. She liked being busy, for sure, but she began to despise her customers, who were not at all interested in making polite conversation or getting to know who she was. It was all 'make mine extra hot, dear', 'don't put lemon in that, love', 'are the scones fresh today?', 'I would prefer the clotted cream on the side'. Years after she opened, it had become a chore. In addition, her husband was not well, and she was diagnosed with early stages of cancer. So when her husband died, and after she sold up, she bought a bottle of Dom Perignon, one crystal flute, then went down to the beach and drank the whole bottle herself. God only knows how she got home. The next week she had bought a one way ticket to Cape Town.

The following week Rachel is waiting for Ivan in the living room of Freedom House. She had poured herself a small sherry, but didn't drink it. She is a little nervous, and a little excited. It is the first time she has been out for such a long time, and to a show she knows nothing about, with a man she knows nothing about. She hears a car pull up and peaks out of the window. Ivan is jumping out of the car and heading to the front door. Before he has time to ring the quaint bell hanging from an old chain, Rachel meets him at the door.

'You look nice,' Ivan says, and immediately looks a little forlorn.

'Thank you, just a little something from the old world,' Rachel replies. Although it isn't entirely true because she had only recently purchased the shawl at Country Road.

'Ready to go? I'm pretty excited to see this show again. Last time I saw 'Chess' was in Melbourne. That would have been in… fuck, no idea. Something from my old world,' Ivan says with a wink.

Rachel steps up to the passenger side seat, and fastens her seat belt. They set off, turning left onto Kloof Nek Road heading toward Table Mountain. Rachel looks out of the window as they drive up the hill. It's a beautiful mild night.

'I was chatting with my girlfriend in London the other night,' Rachel starts inanely, 'You'll meet her soon I hope. She is thinking of coming down for a few weeks. I mean, nothing is set in stone yet, but I'm sure she would love to get here, but more to get out of London for a while. It's funny you know,' Rachel notices that Ivan is concentrating on his driving to an excessive extent. *Is he listening?* She continues her amusing anecdote, continuing to wonder if Ivan is listening and taking it in.

Rachel concludes her story, 'Then she just looked at me and said "I'm never gonna live that down, am I?"'

Ivan laughs out loud.

'I know, right. It's just too funny. I mean, how is that possible?' Rachel says with a degree of pride. *He was listening.* She relaxes and feels confident in a developing friendship. Determined to enjoy the rest of the evening, she looks out to the dark water of Camps Bay and smiles.

It was not long after the opening party that she was invited to William and Annie's house for a Sunday braai. *What a treat*, she thinks to herself as she cheerily drives along the N2 freeway toward the airport to pick up one of her best friends from the UK. Marge has been her closest confidant and friend for many years, sharing the highs, lows, and intimate details of each other's life. Marge had called her only a week ago, saying she needed to get out of 'this fucking city', and that she had some rather upsetting news which she would rather tell her in person than on a Skype call. Rachel knew too well it would be cancer! But the finer details would probably make the visit a little emotionally intense. In any case, Rachel had decided to make her visit as much fun as she could and treat Marge to the spoils of Cape Town. So when Annie asked if she was free for the braai, Rachel asked if she could bring her dear friend from the UK with her. Rachel knew it would not be an imposition, and that both William and Annie enjoyed meeting new people.

It was cancer, of course, and Marge had started chemo and an intense vitamin C therapy. It was all too familiar for Rachel, but wounded soldiers make the best listeners.

Early Sunday afternoon, Rachel gets up from the sizable sofa in the living room of Freedom House, and walks toward the stairs. 'We have to leave soon, Marge,' Rachel yells up the stairwell, vainly directing her statement to Marge's room. Marge's door swings open and she descends the stairs. 'You look fabulous,' Rachel declares. With the chemo, Marge had lost her hair and had opted for an elaborate headdress rather than a wig. 'What a beautiful outfit. You'll turn some heads this afternoon for sure,' Rachel adds. 'It's very you! And I'm guessing very London!'

'Not too much?' Marge questions.

'Not at all. Now we must get going.'

Annie answers the door at their house and warmly hugs Rachel and shakes hands with Marge. She leads them into the garden where William jumps up from his deck chair and gives Rachel a tight hug. She goes a little weak at the knees, and enjoys the moment of being wrapped in the firm arms of a strong man. William releases her and flashes her a smile and a wink. He turns to Marge and gives her a hearty handshake. 'Welcome to our home,' he says. He places his left hand on her upper arm and spends a few seconds examining her outfit, then smiles. Rachel senses William is clearly impressed with Marge's dress sense. *He's a true international gentleman,* Rachel thinks.

'Now, can I get you ladies a drink?' William finally asks.

The 'boyz', as Annie calls them, arrived a bit later, and Rachel is elated that Marge is comfortable chatting with her friends and is able to cast off the dire reality of her cancer for at least a few hours. It's such a beautiful afternoon, Rachel looks around her and is filled with an overwhelming sense of gratitude, 'We must do this more often,' she says.

'Marie was talking about getting together regularly on Wednesdays, to try out new restaurants for lunch,' Annie says. 'She is free most Wednesdays.'

'Would be great for us to get some ideas for our guests,' Kris confirms.

'We're in,' Ayden says, finishing a sip of wine and joining the cause.

'Then that's us all. How exciting,' Rachel adds.

They started the 'Wednesday Lunch Club', on a mission to sample new restaurants each week, primarily as reconnaissance for their respective guesthouses, but they all knew it was a ruse. Moreover, the eight friends, in all permutations, simply enjoyed being with each other to eat, drink, and chat. They had met some amazing chefs, tasted some fabulous and diabolically bad food, tried some of the best wines in South Africa, caused scenes in restaurants, and made waitresses cry or walk out on the job. That was the Lunch Club! All of them had witnessed the fury of Ayden after a few too many drinks, sometimes directed at management or staff, and on one or two occasions, his displeasure was directed at his friends. All is forgiven and is rarely mentioned. Ayden mellowed over the years, for which she was relieved.

For Rachel, despite her Jewish roots, Christmas was the most wonderful time of year. In Cape Town her small circle of friends became her new family, and she was more than likely invited to lunch somewhere. The year that Nelson Mandela died, she was invited to Kris and Ivan's house. It was the year after they had closed their guesthouse and converted it into their own residence - more renovations! A bedroom became a kitchen, a kitchen became a study, another bedroom now a bathroom and closet, the pool was moved, and two outside rooms became a garage. It was exhausting just thinking about it for Rachel.

Christmas lunch is a resplendent spread with great wines and bubbles, and all the trimmings of an English Christmas. Perhaps mostly due to Ayden, who amongst them all was the staunchest steward of these traditions.

'What a wonderful meal.' Rachel announces. 'Thank you. It is always such a delight to be here with you all.'

'Our pleasure to have you here, Rachel.' Kris says.

'Your place next year?' Ayden jokes to Rachel. There are some smiles.

'I wouldn't know where to start.' Rachel says, hoping it's left there.

'It's been a helluva year for this country.' Daniel says, contributing to a conversation which he feels needs to be steered in a different direction. 'I mean we lost Nelson Mandela, then that debacle of a memorial, and worse, the poor man's funeral. Just so little respect.'

Ivan, who was busy warming the brandy sauce, joins them at the table, sauce in hand. 'And that business with Oscar Pistorius in February. I mean does anyone in the country really believe his story about hearing a burglar, not noticing Reeva is not in bed? Asshole.'

Rachel, who is sitting opposite Marie, inadvertently notices her reaction to the comment. She's going to be sick, Rachel thinks, sensing it is almost personal for her.

'We are not going to talk about that, nor him, at the Christmas table, nor on Christmas Day.' Ayden interrupts and promptly puts an end to that conversation. They all know the authoritative voice of Ayden, so his decision goes unchallenged. He picks up his drink and proposes a toast to the hosts, then turns to look to Rachel: 'We'll all pitch in, of course. You just have to host.' He raises his glass. 'To next year at Freedom House.'

Rachel whines 'Oaw no.'

Wiping the urn of sea and salt, Rachel puts it in her wardrobe. She stands there staring at it for some time and begins to cry. *Such a beautiful soul.* Still in disbelief, she can't imagine how things can ever be the same now for any of them - Ayden, Daniel, Kris, Ivan, Annie, and William. Perhaps even more so for poor Pierre. *Pierre! Where is Pierre?* Rachel realises he was not invited to their little ceremony, but more, he hasn't been seen nor heard from since or before the accident. *Perhaps he just couldn't face any of us and went back to France.*

No family to contact, no will, no further instructions. All she had was just left - the apartment, the car. Rachel was told by Ayden that the diamond from her ring was found at the restaurant. That, and a small bronze sculpture, completely disfigured, were the only items that remained. *I guess Pierre took them.*

She dries her eyes and touches the urn, then closes the wardrobe door.

William

Walking out of the gym in Johannesburg, just a short lope from his hotel, William takes a moment, closing his eyes and facing the sun, to reflect on the state of his life. He is still comparatively young. He is comfortably wealthy, courtesy of his savvy investments and business dealings in London and South Africa, and not forgetting the contract in the Middle East, which was extremely lucrative. Additionally, he has the most beautiful girl in the world as his wife. He smiles and begins jogging in the direction of his hotel. Tomorrow is their 10th wedding anniversary, and he has planned a special dinner at Rust en Vrede in the winelands near Cape Town.

As he jogs down the neat footpath, he mentally dissects the details of his morning meeting with the board of directors, taking note of his personal checklist. He stops and grabs his phone from his backpack. 'Hey SIRI, schedule a FaceTime call with Mark next Wednesday at 10am.' Phone in hand, he continues jogging, which turns into a saunter at the entrance of the hotel. He is greeted by the doorman as he opens the impressive glass doors. William walks into the vacuous lobby of white and dark grey marble and makes his way under the tremendous crystal and gold chandelier toward reception, 'Is there a package for me?' he inquires to the attractive young lady behind the counter, dressed in a perfectly fitting corporate uniform, with her blonde hair tied up in a ponytail.

'Let me check for you, sir.' she says as she turns to go into a concealed room behind the massive wall decorated with flowing twists of iron and glass, dimly lit from above and below such that shadow and light playfully embrace the materials, both enhancing and masking their form. 'Here you are, Mr Clarke.' she says upon returning, handing William a small package.

'Thank you, and please remember, it's William. Mr Clarke is my father,' he says with a grin, which develops into a flashy smile. The receptionist smiles, blushes, and bows her head just slightly. William knows he has an effect on women, which he loves, knowing, of course, there is nothing in it, but perhaps more because of his unwavering love for his wife. 'Please arrange a car to the airport for me in an hour.'

Annie is in the kitchen of their spacious Victorian home in Cape Town, sitting at the breakfast bar nibbling on some raw almonds and celery, flicking through the pages of a trashy gossip magazine when William walks in. 'Good flight?' she says as she loses herself in his arms in a warm embrace.

'Not bad. Usual crowd on the plane.' He grabs some nuts from the bowl on the bench and heads to the cupboard for some wine glasses. 'How were things here? Not too lonely without me?' He moves toward Annie and plants a kiss on the top of her head, breathing in her beautiful scent of pure soap and Giorgio Armani's 'Si', as he does. He tingles, delighting in being with her.

'All good. A bit of shopping, a bit of exercise, lunch with Ayden at Marie's place. Same same.' She dumps the magazine in the bin and sits at the breakfast bar, watching William open a bottle of Steenberg sauvignon blanc. He pours two glasses and they chat for a short time. Never about business, just people and the events surrounding his trip to Johannesburg.

He can't explain why, but he is smitten with Annie; she is his reason for being. He has never had a reason to feel guilty, like he has something to hide or to make up to her. He has truly found his soulmate and best friend. God, he knows how corny that sounds, and he would never use either of those phrases in telling her, or anyone else, how much he loves her. It's just that... it's the truth. They have been together for a little over 12 years, and he still adores her, a love which has developed and grown from the day they first met in Medina.

-§-

In his early-to-mid-20s William scored an extremely well-paid contract as an engineer and site manager with a Saudi construction company in Medina. He will always remember fondly the time when, at an expat social gathering in the middle of the desert, he laid eyes on a beautiful Irish girl with blond hair and pale, flawless skin as smooth as porcelain, very fit, and with the energy and effervescence of opening a bottle of soda water after you had shaken it for five minutes. After meeting her, William made it his goal to be with Annie for the rest of his life. His friends advised him that she would be a difficult catch, but after a well-tempered campaign of flowers and small gifts, as if Walt Disney himself had written the story, Annie fell to his charm.

William didn't know much about Annie. He was told she was a spy, under the guise of working for an airline company, but he knew that was a joke, or at least he didn't really care. The thought of falling in love with a spy was thrilling, becoming an international man of mystery, or better, a Bond villain. He did know that there would be plenty of time to get to know each other's stories in the ensuing years together. When the time came for William to finish his contract, he asked Annie to join him back in London. Annie left her job the same day and followed him there. A couple of years later, William popped the question and presented Annie with a ring supporting such an impressive 'rock' that she remarked 'I'll never be able to lift up my hand wearing this.'

-§-

'Don't forget you have invited Ivan and... oh, what is his name?.. you know, for a braai on Sunday.' Annie reminds William.

'Kris!' William says. 'Yup, got it.'

'Such a nice couple of guys, don't you think? I'm glad Marie dragged us back to meet them.'

'We took some convincing, right?

'She can be very persuasive.'

'We were a bit late for our meeting, but glad we met them.'

'And I'm glad you invited them. You're good at reading people.'

'So is Marie, for that matter. They seem like good guys. Kris has a keen interest in the business side of things here. I believe he headed up a pharmaceutical company in South Korea. Anyway, looking forward to chatting with him more.'

'Really? He noticed you flirting with Marie, you know, when you went inside to write down the information for them both.'

'I have no idea what you're talking about.' William leans across to give Annie a playful kiss. 'I'll go to Woolworths tomorrow morning and get some stuff. Beef alright?'

'Sure, and get some salady things. I'll make something up with whatever you bring home. I asked Ayden if they're free, and of course they are, but they can't be here til just before two. They are really 'hands-on' with their guesthouse.' She smiles at William. 'Oh, and Rachel. I asked her as well, and she has a friend from the UK visiting, so she's bringing her.'

'Good, so there's eight of us. Don't forget we're going out for dinner tomorrow night.'

'Oh yeah... what is that for again?'

William wraps his arms around her and lifts her off the floor, 'Because I love you.' He kisses her and sits her on top of the breakfast bar, and runs his warm hands up the back of her t-shirt.

'Oh, and where are we going? Just so I know what to wear.'

'It's a surprise, and... I think you look best with nothing on at all.' He smiles and kisses the side of her neck. 'Besides, you always look amazing, and you have never needed to be told what to wear or how to dress.' William releases Annie, rinses his wine glass and heads to the bedroom at the front of the house. 'I'll unpack then take a shower before dinner.'

William washes the shampoo out of his hair as he stands under the warm stream of water cascading over his broad shoulders, down his chest and back. He thinks about Marie, then thinks, he thinks about Marie a lot. When they first met in her restaurant he knew she was ogling him. He remembers enjoying her eyes scanning him in a very sensual manner, which continues to be the case whenever they meet. He lifts his face toward the shower rose, opens his mouth to take in some warm water, then spits it out. His adoration for, and commitment to, Annie has never wavered, and never will, but he knows if Annie were not on the scene, he and Marie would be having sex whenever and wherever they wanted. He grins, and runs his hand over his chest, and down to his lower body, then back up to his face. William knows the superficial flirting with Marie is just that - superficial. Despite his occasional sexual feelings for other women, he is too much in love with Annie to ever compromise their relationship or hurt her. However, Marie intrigues him; there is more to her than she is willing to share. Perhaps no one really knows her. Maybe that dimwitted brother of hers does, but who could be arsed even trying to get sense out of him? She had come from France, from Lille, he remembers. *But why Cape Town now? Such a long way away. She never talks about going back to see family…nothing!* William turns off the shower and steps out. He catches himself in the mirror. *Not bad. I'm all yours, Annie.*

It's a beautiful Saturday evening in October, William is sitting on the extremely large bespoke couch in their living room, looking at his phone. The couch is too large for the two of them, but it fits the room perfectly. He's found an acceptable semi-casual jacket to wear over an open-neck white shirt, and some expensive dark jeans. There's a small royal-blue velvet box on the sizable coffee table in front of him. 'The car's here.' he sings out. A minute later, Annie waltzes into the room wearing a breathtakingly beautiful ivory toned, fitted, mid-length dress, a slightly darker long sleeve sequined Bolero, and matching heels. Her hair is up and she has a simple dusting of make-up which enhances her high cheek bones and smooth, thin neck. 'Tadaaa!' she sings raucously.

'Wow!' William exclaims. 'You look sensational.' He stands and moves behind her and kisses the nape of her neck, not wanting to interfere with her makeup, and savouring her rich, sweet aroma. He runs his hands down her thighs, enjoying the texture of her dress and the shape of her body. 'Shall we forget dinner and go to bed?' he gently whispers in her ear.

Annie turns and moves her lips to his ear and softly whispers, 'Not a chance BB, not after all the time I've spent getting ready.' She playfully bites his earlobe. William goes weak, reminding him of the unfair advantage Annie often has over him.

He reaches for the small box on the coffee table. 'Happy Anniversary. This is just to say I love you to bits.' He opens the lid to expose a simple yellow gold, thin band ring with a cluster of five small brilliant diamonds, and hands it to Annie.

'Oh, Bill, it's beautiful. So elegant. You really didn't need to do this.' She gives him a kiss, and they embrace warmly for some time. 'I didn't get you anything.'

'Perfect,' he says, and removes the ring from its home and places it on Annie's right hand ring finger. 'I don't need anything more than you.'

Annie wipes some lipstick off William's lips with her fingers, allowing her touch to linger. She smiles at him and a tear begins to well in her eyes. 'I love you,' she says. A car horn sounds from their driveway. He kisses the top of Annie's head and leads her to the door.

Sunday morning, William is in the kitchen preparing some breakfast with a view to taking it to Annie in bed. He doesn't notice her sneaking up behind him, only feeling the warm flesh of her arms wrap around his waist and her hands sliding up his bare chest. 'Good morning,' she says. 'Thank you for a wonderful anniversary.'

'I was planning to bring this in for you - breakfast in bed.'

'We can have it in the garden. It's a beautiful morning.'

William swings around to give Annie a hug. She is wearing only his shirt from last night. 'You look sexy in my clothes.' Annie smiles and blows him a kiss Marilyn Monroe-style as she swings around and heads out to the garden. William stares at her as she leaves, just for a minute, maybe more. He smiles and adjusts himself, recalling their evening together last night.

He finishes cooking, plates up and, donning a t-shirt, brings the plates of breakfast out to Annie. 'Voila! What time is lunch today?'

'I think you said around 1pm.' Annie says as she eyes up the wholesome breakfast. 'I'll toss a salad or two together, and perhaps I should go and buy some fresh bread at Jason's this morning.'

'Yup, great idea.'

'Great Hollandaise, my darling.' She smiles at him.

'We should have invited Marie as well.'

'She's always so busy though.'

'It is hard to find time to catch up with her, I agree.'

'I think she's working extra hours because Pierre is not working there anymore.'

'Really? His choice or hers?' He smiles, knowing the answer already. 'I'll pick up some wine from the hotel cellar this morning. Do you think I have time for the gym?'

'Your choice. You could just opt to relax today.'

William knows what that means, and agrees to help prepare the house for their guests this afternoon.

It has developed into a gorgeous afternoon, warm but not hot, a light breeze from the north, and plenty of sunshine. It is certainly early spring in the garden, with some flowers and bulbs already in bloom, and the deciduous trees budding. Their house is a beautiful Victorian close to the city but with the distinct attraction of having a small walled garden - a private oasis on the corner of the streets. The house itself is large enough for a family with some 5 bedrooms, most with ensuite. A large entrance hall leads to the spacious living room, dining room, and commodious kitchen. At the back, a small pool winds around the corner of the house and looks up to a terrace which extends from the living room, providing a commanding view of both the city and Table Mountain. The house is certainly 'boxed in' with the surrounding properties, but it proudly exudes a charm and status which outshine its rivals.

Staff from the hotel were called in to assist Annie in making the salads and cleaning the house, making it extremely clean instead of just very clean. William smiles as he watches his wife politely direct the staff to different chores, always with the best intentions and care, but coming across a bit like the Lady of the Manor. He had fired up the Weber about an hour ago, allowing the coals to become white hot embers. The fillet steak will only take about twenty-five minutes to cook to a beautiful medium-rare, and he will wait for guests to arrive before he adds it to the grill.

Rachel arrives just after one pm, together with her friend Marge, who is 'from the UK, and is visiting for a month.' Annie leads them both into the garden, and William gives Rachel a big hug and a smile. He knows the effect it has on her, of course, and perhaps even more so, given his simple hand shake to Marge. Annie catches his eye and winks. William places his hand on Marge's shoulder, an attempt to be more warm than just a hand shake, and tries not to stare too much as she has clearly got the dress code wrong, opting for 'fancy-dress' and coming dressed as Norma Desmond - complete with turban, straight off the set of Sunset Boulevard. He smiles anticipating what Ayden will say when he sees her. 'Now, can I get you ladies a drink?'

Kris and Ivan arrive twenty minutes later. Annie brings them into the garden and William offers them each a glass of wine. Kris takes a white and Ivan a red. Annie steals Ivan away for the grand tour of the house, linking her arm in his as she leads him on. Rachel jumps up to meet Kris and introduces him to Marge, 'She is visiting from the UK, staying with me for a month.' Kris, despite being accustomed to meeting all manner of international guests, is somewhat bewildered. William steps in, 'A top-up ladies? Kris, help me in the kitchen, will you?'

'That's quite an outfit,' Kris says with a smirk, 'Did I misunderstand the dress code?'

William laughs, delighted that Kris felt comfortable enough to make the comment. 'I'm in your boat. She's a friend of Rachel's, visiting from the UK.'

'Staying for a month,' Kris finishes the rhetoric.

'Go and top up their glasses, will you? Two white wines.' The doorbell rings. 'That will be Ayden and Daniel. Brace yourself! I have no idea what Ayden will say.'

William meets them at the front door, and leads them to the garden. He chooses not to say anything about Rachel's friend; rather boyishly, he is excitedly anticipating the events as they unfold naturally.

Coming from the kitchen, William brings a glass of red for Ayden and white for Daniel. Daniel is chatting to Rachel and Kris, and true to form, appears to be oblivious to the 'theatre' of Marge. Ayden, by contrast, is completely and utterly besotted with the spectacle, and deep in conversation with her. William hands him his wine, and the two of them catch each other's eye. William sees the glint in Ayden's eye and smiles.

Annie returns with Ivan, who is excessively impressed with the house. William muses perhaps it is more about Ivan's life than the house. Annie and Ivan head over to Ayden, who shakes Ivan's hand, warmly holding his upper arm, then gives Annie a kiss on the cheek. William looks at his group of friends in this part of the world, in his home, and smiles. He is so fortunate, so blessed.

He checks the braai, but his curiosity is killing him. He approaches Ayden. 'Can I borrow you for a moment?' he says, interrupting the conversation. 'I need some advice in the kitchen.'

'Where the fuck did she find that outfit?' Ayden says once he is out of range. 'Interesting soul, but somehow she was absent for the briefing on appropriate attire for 'braai-casual', instead opting for the 'I'm ready for my close up, Mr DeMille' look. Have you seen her nails? Extraordinary!'

William takes a sip of wine and smiles, which, once he has almost swallowed, turns into a laugh. 'I knew you would love her.'

'I mean, for sure everyone has their own style, but fuck me, a gold turban and silk caftan with ochre slippers? Who wears that shit? TO A BRAAI?' Ayden swigs his wine. William watches him, anticipating the second wave. 'And that makeup, for fuck's sake. She can barely hold a glass of wine with those nails, let alone drink from the glass with that thick lipstick. That's if her false lashes don't knock the glass out of her hand first. I mean, Liz Tayler, eat your fuckin' heart out.' The two of them laugh heartily.

Annie wanders into the kitchen, grabs a cloth to wipe her t-shirt, then sidles up to William, who throws his arms around her and kisses the top of her head.

'Please tell me you didn't leave Ivan alone with Cleopatra,' Ayden says with alarm.

'Oh, he's doing fine,' Annie says.

'It's time I put my meat on the braai.' William says, smiling and moving toward the tray on the bench.

'I think there's a line there…' Ayden jests.

-§-

William has a soft spot for Ayden. He likes his sense of humour, his quick wit, and unashamed brashness, which some find offensive, but he knows Ayden couldn't care less. Or as Ayden would say 'doesn't give a shit!' It was Ayden who gave him the nickname Buffalo Bill, whilst at a party, Annie sang 'You Can't Get a Man With a Gun' from the old Irving Berlin musical. Annie loved the nickname so much she frequently refers to him as BB.

The four of them met in Marie's restaurant quite a few months ago. Perhaps it was over a year ago now. It seems quite normal to make new friends in Marie's place; it's that sort of restaurant, and Marie is the grand hostess of making connections.

William remembers the beautiful day in December. He is opening a bottle of white wine. Annie is chatting to Marie about the lunch menu when two guys, similarly dressed in dark trousers and matching blue shirts, waltz into Serge's heading for what William assumed was 'their' table. Clearly they had been there several times before. William notices the sideways glance from them both, and the subsequent nod of approval of his physique. He smiles, as well as perhaps puffing up his chest a little more, as he opens the bottle.

'You're such a flirt,' Annie declares, with a big, proud, smile.

Marie squeezes William's shoulder, 'You have to meet these guys. They own a guesthouse in Oranjezicht. From the UK.' Marie gestures to the couple, and they make their way over, with some haste.

'You haven't met yet,' Marie states, 'William and Annie, Daniel and Ayden.'

William stands and, exerting his masculinity, shakes Ayden's hand, then Daniel's, knowing they would appreciate his strength, in response to their glances of approval.

'Wow, that's a firm grip.' Ayden says with a wry smile.

William catches Annie's eye, and they smile. 'Come and join us. We haven't eaten yet, but we have just opened a bottle of Cederberg sauvignon blanc.'

'Well, it would be rude not to,' Ayden replies.

William watches Annie, knowing she would be sizing them both up, remaining protective of herself until she felt comfortable enough to relax with new people. She had mellowed since they first met, and William smiles knowingly. Annie nods to them both, as they take their seat. Marie returns to the table with a small container of ice and ice tongs, and two glasses. Annie takes a cube and drops it into her glass of wine.

'So, where are you kids from, and what are you doing here?' Ayden starts.

William pours wine in the two extra glasses. He likes the bold approach from Ayden, already warming to him. He is a solid looking guy, perhaps even a bit stocky. Piercing eyes and a strong face. Not tall, but generally in proportion, with large shoulders and chest. His hands were also quite large, but William noted a slight weakness in his grip.

He looks at Daniel, who, like Annie, is a little more reserved. He has a strong, intelligent face and is deep in thought. *Quite possibly a bit on the spectrum*, William thinks. A good head of dark brown hair, but not particularly in any style. Daniel is clearly a little more in shape than Ayden with strong shoulders and good arms. His eyes, though, are more glassy, more contemplative, more 'elsewhere'.

'It's an extremely long and boring story,' Annie says, 'one which I'm sure William will fill you in on... on another occasion. However, in a nutshell, we own a rather beautiful set of properties, of which the main house is around the corner - it's a tiny hotel - for the discerning traveller,' she adds with a wink.

'How fab!' Ayden replies.

-§-

William sharpens his knife on the Zwilling steel and starts to carve the fillet. It looks and smells fantastic, and he smiles at his prowess on the braai. He steals a small piece of meat which didn't make it to the serving plate and throws it in his mouth to confirm his accomplishment. 'I saw that,' Annie says, collecting the salads from the fridge and taking them into the dining room. She returns for the meat platter just as William's mobile phone rings. 'It's Murphy's Law,' she says. William takes off to answer the call, hoping it will be straightforward.

In the dining room with the French doors open to the garden, the lunch guests, still engrossed in conversation, arrive to an impressive spread: fillet steak, boiled potatoes with homemade mayonnaise, red quinoa salad, and a large bowl of baby spinach with red onion, Ricotta and olive oil. 'There's enough to feed an army,' Rachel declares as William arrives at the table after answering the phone call.

'Never let it be said you leave our home hungry,' Annie retorts, as she takes her seat.

'Enjoy!' William states with the confidence of a lord entertaining his guests.

'Anything important?' Annie inquires.

Making light of it in front of their friends, William replies, 'Sometimes it makes you wonder why you have a manager for your hotel, right? A French client wants to stay longer and wants to move into a bigger suite. It's not that difficult. Do we have one available? Is he happy with the new price? Then make it happen.'

'Is he the well-dressed man?' Annie asks.

'Sounds like it. He has stayed with us on several occasions, and each time he stays a bit longer. An interesting chap.'

'Mmm, he's very good looking. But not as handsome as my Bill.' Annie says as she passes the bowl of spinach across the table.
People laugh, and get back to the business of eating.

William tries to brush aside his instinctual unease relating to the phone call. He knows why his manager called him, and he is certainly not comfortable with the continual visits and unknown dealings of the French guest. He is not a tourist, and he is not here for business. Each stay for a longer time, never meeting or seeing anyone, just lurking in the streets of Cape Town, almost waiting for something to happen. Always paying with cash, which he brings with him from Europe, it would seem. William wonders whether he should talk to the man, offer assistance, find out more about him. He has been coming for just over a year now, and not on a regular, routine basis. Seemingly ad hoc.

He returns his focus to his guests, enjoying having the people he has begun to have affection for at his table, feeling like they are his old friends. Rachel with her stories of The Little Tea Room and her late husband. Ayden and Daniel, always quick with a joke or an anecdote, which at first might seem superficial, but with an undisputed deep warmth. Kris and Ivan, the new kids on the block, an interesting couple of two individuals, both of them evoking in William a natural desire to embrace wholeheartedly. He looks across the table at Annie as she delights their guests with another story. He smiles. She is weaker now than when they first met; he knows that's true, and so does she, although she will never concede. The disease is slowly but surely destroying the woman he loves so dearly.
He catches the end of Annie's anecdote, '...well, I just couldn't decide on diamonds or tanzanite, so I asked Bill if he would get both put in the necklace.' Annie shows off the necklace he had bought her last year for their anniversary.
'Of course he did,' Ayden says, smiling with amusement.
William smiles at Annie then, lifting his glass, charges a toast, 'To good friends.' He discreetly wipes a tear from his eye.

Daniel

'Please tell me you're not making me do this.' Daniel says with a shy smile. He is, of course, extremely curious, and a little excited, but is never one to make a scene or, in this case, an entrance.

'You'll be fine. Apparently he's a lovely guy and very good looking,' Sam says as she drags Daniel toward the office door, evidently against his will.

'How do you know this guy?' Daniel inquires.

'I don't. My best friend does. She was employed a few times through this agency, so she knows him. She says it's 'all thumbs up' for him, and you need all the bloody help you can get when it comes to meeting guys. If we can't find someone for you then no one can.' She stops outside the office door, dramatically trying to calm Daniel down and fussing over his look, brushing down his tailored suit and straightening his silk tie.

'Don't touch my hair,' Daniel says in exasperation, responding to the excited nervousness in his friend.

'Shut up.' Sam grabs his arms and holds them to his side. 'Now listen, he's from 'Norn Ireland'. He owns this company and has been in London a few years. He's very good looking AND,' she breathes, 'terribly single... Are you ready?'

'No.'

'Let's do this.'

As Sam eases open the frosted glass doors of 'Hire Intelligence Staff', Daniel feels like he is in a movie when everything goes pale white. He is delirious with excitement and fear in equal measure, well, perhaps not that equal. They approach the receptionist, a dim-witted-looking lad. *Ironic,* Daniel thinks to himself, given the name of the company. Sam tries to attract his attention, but he is busy typing something which is clearly very, very, very important. Finally he looks up to Sam and Daniel. Sam begins, 'Is Mr...' but before she finishes her request, a door from down the corridor, past the plush waiting room, swings open. Sam steps aside as Daniel stares at the tall, confident gentleman approaching the reception desk.

'He's taller than I thought,' Daniel says.

'Me too,' Sam confirms.

'But you're right, very handsome.'

He walks up to the reception desk, looks at Daniel, and smiles.

'Same time next month, Mr Steale?' The dizzy receptionist asks. The gentleman nods and the receptionist schedules the appointment, making the process look more difficult than it ought. Mr Steale smiles at Sam and Daniel, walks past them both, and heads out the door.

As they watch him leave, Daniel feels the wind has blown out of his sails. Utterly exhausted and deflated from the false alarm, he grabs Sam's arm, ready to leave. He turns to her, then notices the very good-looking man sporting a fantastic light grey suit with a darker grey, open-neck shirt and a devilish smile, walking down the corridor toward them.

'Feckin' accountants,' he says. 'You can't live with 'em and you can't live without 'em. Hi, I'm Ayden. You must be Daniel.'

-§-

From 'his' immaculate penthouse apartment in Cape Town, looking out toward the harbor, Daniel smiles remembering the first time he met Ayden. It's Wednesday morning, and the sun is starting to burn off the remnants of the sea fog sitting in the harbor, making the cranes of the port look like giraffes sticking their heads out of the mist. He sips his English Breakfast tea from a bone china teacup. He and Ayden hit it off in a very real way, and within a year they had shacked up together in London's Kensington. They both had great jobs and a significant disposable income; they were young-ish and free of other commitments; they enjoyed life. Except, ultimately, they both felt there had to be more to life than that in London, and the search for new pastures lead them to the shores of Cape Town.

He finishes his tea, rinses his cup and leaves it in the sink, then pushes down the lever of the fire-engine-red SMEG toaster, lowering the bread into the cavity, the elements already glowing. Absentmindedly, he collects the butter from the Union Jack painted SMEG fridge, and Marmite from the pantry cupboard. He would have to be in the guesthouse in a couple of hours. His shift starts well after breakfast service, to ensure he is out of Ayden's way, and just in time to chat with and advise their guests as they head out for the day. Thereafter he checks the online bookings, emails, and all the admin for the business that Ayden doesn't do. They have worked out their roles in a rather organic way, and they are both very happy with that.

Daniel checks the oversized novelty clock on the wall. *Plenty of time,* he thinks.

He loves 'his' apartment, and as much as he loves Ayden, the two of them enjoy their time apart. When they had first bought the guesthouse, the two of them lived together in the only ground floor guest room with the view that one day they would buy an apartment to get out of the house. But when they found the perfect place, Ayden decided to stay in the extra guest room of the large house, and the apartment, or 'the sink estate' as Ayden calls it, referring to the socially challenged council estates in the UK, became Daniel's escape.

He settles on the couch with his toast and adjusts the novel he has been reading for the last few days, so that the spine is parallel to the edge of the table. It was a gift from Annie for his birthday. She thought it would interest him given that both his parents were involved in The Royal Ballet in London. He remembers so many fantastic nights as a child, with his fraternal twin sister, Qiana, sitting in the wings of the Royal Opera House watching their mum dance, the smell of fresh cigarette smoke still lingering in the stage legs. He was fortunate enough to have grown up with an appreciation of live theatre, for which he would always be grateful to his parents. The downside of his experiences, as it turns out, is that nothing really measures up to professional theatre in London, making the 'arts' scene in Cape Town, for him, quite a bit like 'amateur hour'. Granted, he has been taken by Ivan to a number of great musicals and operas here. Maybe his standards are dropping.

Daniel likes spending time with Ivan and Kris. They have become for him, and for Ayden, he suspects, very special friends. They have seen some beautiful parts of the world together on holiday and spent many nights talking 'shit', or philosophising about the ridiculous outcome of the Eurovision Song Contest, after drinking too much red wine. He smiles and takes a bite of toast.

Daniel thrives on structure and routine, which is part of the reason his life works so well with Ayden. He knows that after the guests have left, after the admin of the morning is completed, and once Ayden is happy with the way the staff are carrying out their duties, (Both Daniel and the staff know there is only one way to clean and make beds, and that is Ayden's way!) the two of them go out for lunch - every day. It's a ritual they both enjoy. It's time to be together, if not always engaged in the same conversation, and a chance to be away from 'work'. They spend a lot of time at Marie's Serge's restaurant, both because the food is consistently good and because they have grown fond of Marie after first meeting her in what was then her new restaurant.

-§-

Despite the risk of encountering the invasive, awkward male waiter again, Ayden and Daniel go back to Serge's for a second time. The food was good last time, and it's generally quiet; moreover it has the charm of a French bistro. They sit at the same table, in the alcove to the left of the entrance. *No sign of the waiter, that's a relief*, Daniel thinks. A young girl comes to take their order. Daniel requests the chicken korma and leaves it up to Ayden to order the wine, knowing he will probably only drink a glass from the bottle. He retrieves his phone from his manbag, opens it, and starts to check 'stuff'. 'Bookings are looking good for the season so far,' Daniel shares to open a dialogue. 'I mean, given we are not on any booking sites, or South African promotion sites, I think we're doing well.'

'I guess there's always room for improvement,' Ayden replies, absently on his phone.

'Sure, I agree. I think we have a very unique offering in the city, and I guess we have to wait until our guests have written reviews and we get the reputation we are looking for.'

'Yup.'

Daniel goes back to his phone, realising Ayden is not in the mood for a chat. Lunch proceeds in a very quiet but relaxed manner.

After the lunch plates are removed, Daniel looks across the street and sees a small black car turn left onto Union Street. *That's a wide turn. I hope there's no one coming from the other direction.* He goes back to his phone, not hearing Ayden gasp. Later, two women walk into the restaurant. The first is short and a little flustered, wearing a smart, light floral dress, and flat shoes. She looks at them both and smiles. The second lady is tall and elegant, with striking facial features, fantastic red lipstick and beautiful dark hair tied up in a ponytail. They move toward the opposite side alcove, chat a little, then the elegant lady goes into the kitchen, returning moments later with a cup of tea. 'I'm guessing she's the owner,' Daniel says.

'What?' Ayden says putting his wine down and coming back to reality.

'The tall lady, I think she's the owner. She's just come out of the kitchen with a cup of tea for the other lady.'

'Good looking lass, for sure. Is she the driver of that black Polo?'

'Shh, I'm trying to eavesdrop on their conversation.'

'Whatev.' Ayden takes a sip of wine then tops up his glass from the bottle.

'Oh my god, another guesthouse owner, I think. Shh… The short lady, she owns a guesthouse, and she's from the UK.'

'Aha.'

'They're getting ready to leave. Don't stare at them.'

'What the hell are you talking about?'

The short lady rushes out of the door, smiling at Daniel as she leaves.

'I'm going to introduce myself. You stay and pay the bill,' Daniel instructs, and runs out of the restaurant.

'Excuse me, pardon me,' Daniel calls out to the lady, trying not to sound alarmist.

The lady spins around. 'Oh, hello, did I leave something behind? Did I drop something on the street? I must be more careful.'

'No, no. Sorry to startle you. I'm just in Serge's and couldn't help overhear your conversation with the owner. You mentioned that you're from the UK and that you have a guesthouse.'

'Oh, yes.'

'Sorry, I'm Daniel.'

'No need to be sorry,' she says.

Daniel stares at her wondering why she said that. Surely she knew that he didn't mean he was really sorry! For what? His name? Was it a joke, perhaps? *Weird.*

'Hi, Daniel, I'm Rachel. Yes, I have Freedom House, on De Lorentz Street.'

'OK, well we have literally just started business at our guesthouse in Oranjezicht, Montrose Manor. It would be great, if it's OK with you, to catch up one day and, you know, compare notes, so to say. Perhaps we could arrange to have lunch one day at Serge's.' Daniel finds a business card in his spacious manbag. 'Here are our contact details,' handing her the card, 'literally straight off the press.' He smiles.

Rachel looks at the card, 'Ayden and Daniel. Are you a couple?'

'For lack of a better term, yes, we are.'

Her smile fades ever so slightly. 'That would be absolutely splendid,' she says. 'Wonderful to meet you, and I look forward to meeting again and being introduced to your man.'

Daniel smiles briefly at Rachel as she turns to head into the supermarket. She is an interesting lady, quite petite. *Good legs, boobs, and arse*, he decides. Immaculate auburn hair that looks as if there's never been a hair out of place. *She could do with a bit of a makeover. Then she'd almost be a knockout.*

He jogs back into Serge's, very pleased with himself, to find Ayden talking to the tall lady.

'…And him, what's plodding back in here, is Daniel,' Ayden says to the lady by means of a sloppy introduction.

'What?' Daniel says, disbelieving what Ayden said.

'This is Marie. French, I believe, or am I mistaking the accent?' Ayden asks.

'Oui, tu as raison, enchantée.' Marie offers her hand to Daniel.

Daniel takes her hand in his, admiring her long sensual fingers and beautiful nail polish. He mock kisses the dorsal of her hand. 'A great pleasure to meet you, Marie. We like your restaurant. We have a guesthou…'

'Done all that!' Ayden interrupts abruptly.

Daniel huffs. *He's so gruff sometimes.*

Marie smiles warmly. A smile that reminds Daniel of his late mother.

Ayden packs up his things. 'Right, time to go. I'll fill you in on the way home.'

Daniel pushes his chair under the table. He smiles at Marie and mouths the words 'thank you' to say goodbye.

'Nice to meet you again, Marie, and we will see you soon,' Ayden continus. 'Oh, by the way, your male waiter... don't mean to be rude, but he could do with some more training.'

In the Daimler, Ayden drives down Kloof street, past the restaurant, and turns right onto Union Street. Daniel can hear him talking but is too lost in his own thoughts to really register any information. He looks out of his passenger window and notices a dark haired, handsome man dressed in a well-tailored dark suit and an open-neck chambray shirt, leaning against a wall chatting on his mobile. *Mmmm, sexy daddy*, he thinks.

'Are you listening to me?' Ayden says, breaking Daniel's daydream.

-§-

In hindsight, after so many years, it seemed to Daniel they had met nearly everyone of importance at Serge's. It was that kind of bistro, and Marie was so good at reading people and knowing if they would all get on. He takes the last bite of toast and takes the plate to the sink, then, staring at his hand, begins to account for the friends they had met at Serge's, checking them off with his fingers: *Marie, Rachel, Annie and William, Kris and Ivan. That's it, I think. Oh, and Janine and James... but maybe they're not as important... perhaps to Marie.* He smiles knowingly and looks at the clock again. *OK, time for a shower.* He fastidiously washes the few items in the sink, leaving them to dry on the drainer. Before heading to the bathroom, he meticulously wipes down the bench and sink with the dish cloth, then dries his hands on the white hand towel, replacing it, folded, on the towel rail. His phone pings. It's a WhatsApp from Ivan asking if they're available for Lunch today.

Yup.

Where ya wanna go?

Serge's?

Yup .

No new ideas then.

I'll check with A for a time and
a new idea when I get to
the GH and get back to you.

It's 10.30 already,
why are you not at work?

Fuck off. I'm about to
take a shower now now

Daniel in the shower,

Be still my heart.

Don't 'shake your spear' at me.

-§-

Daniel had seen Kris and Ivan several times in Serge's, looking so busy on their laptops. Both he and Ayden had dismissed them as a couple of tossers, with too much time and money to have real jobs. Today, as they drove past the restaurant, he saw them again inside. 'They're there again,' he says to Ayden, not realising he was speaking quite softly in case the two guys inside the restaurant heard him.
'Why are you whispering?' Ayden asks incredulously. 'They can't hear you!'

After parking the car further up the street, Daniel and Ayden, with some haste, head into the restaurant, taking their usual table. Daniel tries not to stare at the two guys, but knows he is hopelessly curious. Marie strides over to them, bottle of Hartenberg cabernet sauvignon and two glasses in hand, ready to chat.

'So, they're here again?' Daniel says.

'They're here most days.' Marie replies. 'They bought The Lady Hamilton, and are in the middle of major renovations - remodeling the inside completely, all new bathrooms, redoing the floors, repainting the whole place. Lots of work, eh?'

Daniel tunes out of the conversation, thinking, *The Lady Hamilton?*

'Wait a minute,' Daniel interrupts, 'you said they have started renovations? At The Lady Hamilton?'

'Mmm,' Marie confirms.

'But I can see The Lady Hamilton from the sink estate, and there is absolutely no sign of renovations going on... at all!'

Daniel tunes out again, rethinking and, ultimately, justifying his statement. He finds himself blindly staring at one of the laptops. 'Is that a black MacBook? I haven't seen one like that before.'

Ayden stares at him, 'What?'

Daniel continues to look vaguely in the direction of the two guys, trying not to stare. He thinks they're both attractive. He wonders what age they are and whether they are part of a larger consortium with money that is planning to start renovations. Maybe Marie has just got the whole story wrong. He notices one of the guys getting up from their table. He is attractive for sure, not tall, nor short. Shortish light brown hair and good shoulders. Perhaps not as broad as himself, but certainly he has spent some time in the gym. A well-proportioned face that could frighten a rival or welcome a friend, a great square chin. 'Shh... one of 'em's coming.'

'Hi, I'm Kris.'

Daniel looks back to see the other guy still busy on his black MacBook. *What is he doing that is so important, that he can't come and introduce himself as well?*

'The Lady Hamilton? No, no, The Lady Victoria,' Kris reveals.

'Ahhh... Where the fuck is that?' Ayden exclaims.

Ayden - always the charmer, Daniel thinks.

-§-

Daniel tip-toes out of the shower, trying not to make too much mess with the water. He grabs his towel and steps back into the shower cubicle to dry off.

He remembers it was initially a bit of a rocky road with Kris and Ivan. They seemed a little aloof, and there was the mess-up with their invitation to the opening of the Victoria Boutique Villa, as in, Daniel and Ayden weren't invited. Kris had called them on the day of the party explaining what had gone wrong, and whilst Daniel was happy to go, Ayden had excused them both, claiming they were not a 'rent-a-crowd'. It didn't stop them driving by Victoria Boutique Villa that evening to have a gander. Daniel thought it looked amazing, lit up like a Christmas tree. It was that night that Daniel saw the same handsome man he had seen on Union Street about two months ago. He was standing under a tree just up Bath Street looking at the house. Daniel looked at the house to see what the man was so interested in, and when he looked back he had gone.

Strange! he thinks as he continues to vigorously dry his hair.

Within a couple of weeks, the four of them had started meeting regularly and the mishap with invites and opening parties was forgiven and forgotten.

Grabbing his manbag as he leaves the apartment, Daniel double checks he has everything he needs. He closes and locks the door, then checks it three more times to ensure it's locked. He takes the lift down to the lobby and walks a few meters to his car. He likes his car, a 1994 Audi 80 Cabriolet, the same make and model as Princess Diana. He had bought it new in London and couldn't part with it when they moved to Cape Town, so it came with them. Now it needed some major repairs of the canopy, but

Daniel couldn't be bothered; he only drives it to work, to lunch, to the gym, and back home.

His phone pings, another WhatsApp from Ivan.

> Have you left the sink estate yet?
>> I'm in the car. Leave me alone.
> Did you turn off the iron?
>> I didn't use the iron.

Daniel gets out of the car, locks the car door, checks it's locked, then takes the lift back to his apartment, opens the door, and goes to the linen closet to check the iron is unplugged. 'Bastard!' he says out loud.

Driving out of the car park, he turns left, then right, straight up the hill, then left onto Montrose Avenue. *Of course,* he thinks, *it was obvious for Ivan to mention trying a new restaurant - it's Wednesday!* He remembers the Wednesday Lunch Club, which kind of officially started shortly after a braai at William and Annie's house, the day he first met Marge, *such an interesting and articulate lady.*

The eight of them had enjoyed several fantastic lunches at some amazing restaurants. For Daniel, the Lunch Club seriously served its purpose; on the whole, the 'research' was beneficial. He was able to confidently advise their guests about the best, and the less-than-best, places to eat. However, he suspects it became just another drunken party for the rest of the troupe, including Ayden. It was a fun afternoon, and he looked forward to the next each week. However, there were times he just wanted to die, when Ayden had launched an assault of verbal abuse at some poor, young, inexperienced waitron, or at management. He had calmed down so much in the last few years, for which Daniel was relieved.

He parks his car outside the guesthouse, double checks the door is locked, and saunters into the house with a slight air of executive authority. He still, at times, misses his life in London. Certainly the money. He bee lines for the office and turns on the computer. *Why don't we have a laptop?* he thinks.

The old machine winds itself up and starts the day with a grand jingle, which Daniel surmises was written by some lackey at Microsoft. He fusses with papers on the desk and once he is satisfied, he heads down to the kitchen to see Ayden. 'Morning.'

Ayden doesn't look up from tidying the kitchen. 'Those fuckers in room 2, I tell you what. If they leave their room like that again, I'll have to say something. It's a fuckin' pig sty. Morning, my love.' Ayden gives Daniel a rub on the back.

'Who's left in the house?' Daniel inquires.

'Rooms 1, 3, and 4.'

'They're a nice couple, Room 4.'

'He's from Scotland and she's from South Carolina, I believe. Nice people. They have two kids as well.'

'Really?' Daniel remembers his WhatsApp message. 'Ivan wants to know if we're free for lunch. I said yes. Perhaps we can just go back to Serge's.'

'Great. Would be good to catch up with them again. It's been a while, and I'm keen to hear about Kris's new exhibition. I hope Marie's there.'

'She's been so edgy lately. Like she's seen a ghost or something. Ever since Oscar Pistorius killed his girlfriend, she has been really freaked out. It has affected her for some time now.'

'I guess most people think if it can happen to Reeva, it can happen to them. I don't know. In any case, Serge's it is, two o'clock.'

Kris and Ivan are already in the restaurant when Ayden and Daniel arrive.

'Tell me you didn't drive here,' Ivan says, as he gives Daniel a big hug.

'Of course we drove. I have to be back on time. We have real jobs,' Daniel confirms.

'Have you ordered wine yet?' Ayden asks.

'Not yet. We thought we'd leave that up to you,' Kris says.

They settle into the alcove, left of the entrance, and look around. Marie springs out of the kitchen and immediately heads in their direction, despite there being other patrons in need of service. 'How lovely to see you all again; it's been such a long time.'

'I guess we're all busy,' Kris offers.

Daniel smirks and looks at Ivan.

'I am managing a rather successful foundation, thank you very much,' Ivan jumps in, feigning offense.

'Is that still there?' Ayden remarks and laughs.

'It keeps him out of my hair,' Kris jests.

'And off the streets. How times have changed. I guess you're making more money now,' Ayden continues.

'I enjoyed your fundraising cabaret last month,' Daniel adds, not wanting to maintain the light-hearted gibing.

'Thanks. It was fun, eh?' Ivan responds. 'It worked out well for the foundation.'

Marie, who had left the table, returned now with a bottle of Hartenberg cabernet sauvignon and four glasses. 'I'll be back in a minute. I have to serve the other guests.' Marie hands Ayden the corkscrew.

Ayden immediately lays siege on the bottle, 'Don't rush, we have the wine.'

'Have you heard from William and Annie lately?' Kris asks.

'I got a WhatsApp from Annie yesterday, actually,' Daniel says. 'They are planning to be here again next month. BB has some work to do in Joburg, and Annie plans to loaf around Cape Town for a week, before they both head to Sabi Sands.'

'That's the good life, for sure,' Ivan replies. 'We never learned why Annie calls William BB.'

'Seriously? It was Ayden's nickname,' Daniel starts.

Ayden takes over, 'It was at a party years ago, with a bunch of queens, and one of them starts playing the piano, you know, a couple of show tunes, and classic Barbra, etc. Annie is sitting on the stool next to the very cute guy playing piano and she whispers in his ear. Next thing we know she is standing next to the piano and belting out 'You Can't Get a Man With a Gun', you know from Annie Get Your Gun. Great song, great lyrics. 'For a man may be hot, but he's not, when he's shot, Oh, you can't get a man with a gun."

'Anyway,' Daniel continues, 'Once Annie had finished her rendition, Ayden yells out, in his inebriated best, 'With those guns, he's got me.' To screams of laughter from the throng of queens.'

'Then I toasted William and Annie, 'to our Annie, and her Buffalo Bill - our BB',' Ayden concludes.

'Great story,' Kris says, still smirking.

'Although my version of BB for William is Big Boy,' Daniel adds.

Ivan shoves his fingers in his ears, and closes his eyes, 'la, la, la, la, I don't need to hear this.'

'Time for something to eat, and perhaps a second bottle,' Ayden says, attracting Marie's attention, lifting his empty glass. She smiles at Ayden with affection, grabs a bottle from behind the bar, and heads toward the table.

'How are you boys doing?' Marie says, a devilish smirk on her face, as she starts to open the bottle. She looks up and out into the street, her face changes dramatically. 'Oh no, no, oh fock, please NO!' The opened bottle smashes on the floor. Her knees fail her, and she starts to fall, grabbing Daniel's shirt as she plummets. Ayden jumps up and grabs Marie's arms. Ivan clears some chairs and makes space for her. Daniel looks out into the street. *What did she see?* Marie has passed out. Daniel watches Ivan test vital signs. He steps over the ledge of the alcove and looks across the street in time to see the attractive man he had seen before, briskly walking toward the shopping centre.

Kris jumped the ledge, joining Daniel outside. 'I've seen him before. He bought a sculpture from the gallery.'

Annie

Staring out of the window toward the Thames from their beautiful penthouse apartment in Pimlico, London, Annie sighs and caresses her cup of coffee. It's raining again, of course. She has decided to remain positive despite her condition, but watching the rain and grey days in London makes it so difficult. In any case, tomorrow, William and she are going back to Cape Town, where she feels at home. William has some work-related activities in Joburg, and they are going to one of their game reserves after that. The schedule affords her some time to catch up with friends in Cape Town, bathe in the sun, and fundamentally enjoy life.

None of her friends or acquaintances know she has MS, and she tries very hard to shield the signs of decay from them all. Continuing to be the 'belle of the ball', with a witty anecdote or a song. With all due respect, her gay party friends are too busy having a good time to notice the nuances in her behaviour, and as for the staff, she keeps them busy and on their toes. Her close friends also don't know, but she suspects 'the boyz' - Ayden and Daniel, and Kris and Ivan - have noticed something different in her, but they are all too gentlemanly to say anything. Well, Daniel and Ivan can't see past William in any case. She smiles and pulls the cashmere rug, resting on her knees, a little higher.

She knows that Rachel has been through hell with her cancer, and it seems obvious to Annie that Rachel would make the perfect confidant. Yet, not. There has always been something strained about their relationship, and that something is almost impossible to discern. Annie figures both of them are comfortable with their level of friendship. They are there for each other if it's really necessary, but they will never be each other's BFF. They have known each other for the longest time, long before any of the 'others' had even arrived in Cape Town. William and she were looking at investment properties and had decided on making Cape Town their second home. Rachel was mentioned to them by a couple of guys who had recently sold their guesthouse to her, after William had turned it down. So they decided to meet for a coffee at a very cute French-inspired cafe they found on Kloof Street. Manna Epicure was only a stroll away from a property they had just purchased. Rachel arrived wearing a delightfully plain summer frock and flat shoes, which made Annie feel like she was severely overdressed. William delighted them both with stories and jokes, and the occasional accidental flexing of his biceps, as he gesticulated to emphasise his story. It was very clear that Rachel had fallen under his spell, like most girls he met. Annie tended to turn inward on such occasions, both because she was always a little cautious with new people, and because she was comfortable with William being the main attraction. She offered a few light hearted anecdotes during the meeting, but does recall the bemused look, which turned into a look of trepidation, she got from Rachel when she jested about a large girl coming into the cafe, 'You don't want to knock her beer over at a party.' *She missed the joke,* Annie thinks. They were never really on the same page.

Annie gets up from the seat by the window and takes her cup to the kitchen. It's still morning, and she has a few errands to run, and has to pack before tomorrow's late flight. In reality she has plenty of time, so she picks up her iPad and nestles into the long couch in the living room. There is an email from Ivan, wishing them a safe trip tomorrow, and an email from Daniel wishing her the same and saying that there was some news about Marie that he would wait to tell her in person, AND could she get him some UK goss magazines.

The comment about Marie concerns Annie. *What could possibly have happened?* Marie was one of the few women that Annie enjoyed spending time with. She was strong, articulate, and a self-made woman. She also had a mysterious side which intrigued Annie. Over the years, Marie's demeanor had changed. She was once outgoing and full of energy, but at the Christmas Day lunch at Kris and Ivan's place, she was more insular, less courageous. It was the year that Nelson Mandela died, and that horror story of Oscar Pistorius.

They had met Marie only a month or two after meeting Rachel. It was Rachel's suggestion, via text, to try the new restaurant called Serge's on

Kloof Street, and to be sure to meet the owner, a French lady called Marie. So one delightfully sunny day, William and Marie dropped into Serge's as instructed.

-§-

Sitting in the alcove to the right of the entrance, Annie and William are approached by a very striking, tall lady, with beautiful, jet-black hair, tied up in a ponytail. Her face is bright, even animated, accentuated by her dark eye liner and her red lipstick, which scream sex appeal. She is wearing a beautiful, patterned, light wrap-around dress, and, Annie notices, very little else. Annie reaches for William's knee under the table and gives it a squeeze… just a reminder she was still here.
'Hello, I'm Marie,' she says with confidence.
'Hi. I'm William, or Bill, and this beautiful lady is Annie, my wife,' William responds.
'We were advised to come here by a friend of yours, Rachel,' Annie says.
'Oh, how very kind of her. It's a village here, as I guess you already know,' Marie says, almost laughing, and putting her hand on William's shoulder.
Annie watches the obvious chemistry develop between Marie and her husband as they chat and laugh about nothing. She has seen it before, and she has grown to appreciate it, maybe even enjoy the spectacle. It never bothers her because she knows William's heart. She squeezes his knee again. 'Perhaps a bottle of good wine to start,' she suggests.

-§-

In Terminal 5, Heathrow, Annie leaves most of the arrangements up to William; he knows his way around the airport very well. Despite her many years of international flights, both on her own and with William, Annie doesn't like plane travel, but she knows it's a necessary evil. She is grateful that she 'turns left' in the plane, and keeps walking to the front. The staff on BA are usually very good and attentive. She has even come to recognise a few of them, and they her. She also suspects, well, is very certain, that she has been to a few parties in Cape Town with one or more of the flight attendants present. She smiles as she remembers the night at a party, in one of those obscene modern, concrete bunker homes, overlooking the ocean, in Camps Bay, that she sang to William, You Can't Get a Man With a Gun. She sat at the piano with Lucas; a masterful pianist, and decided to surprise William with a song. It was Lucas's idea to sing that song to see if William would blush. He didn't, but the song went down a treat. Ayden and Daniel were there that night, she remembers, and Ayden came up with the nickname for William - Buffalo Bill. Annie chuckles.

Despite her fit appearance, she knows that parts of her body don't work as they used to, and she reminds herself to remain positive, even as she takes her glass of champagne with a shaking hand.

She smiles thinking about Ivan's story about flying first class for the first time. He had told her the story when she was showing him around their house when they came for a braai. He remarked about the size of their place, and how it was a bit overwhelming like the time he was flying back to Australia and had been upgraded to first class on Emirates. *Ya gotta love that Aussie boy.* William walks up behind her and wraps his arms around her waist. 'Love you,' he says and kisses the nape of her neck. Annie turns around and smiles at him with a warmth that conveys her love, gratitude, and need for him. 'What were you thinking about?' William asks.

'Ivan, such a cute guy,' Annie replies.

'That's OK, as long as you're only thinking about cute gay guys.' William winks and smiles at her, a special smile she believes is reserved only for her. She puts her head on his chest just for a moment.

After the plane takes off, Annie sits on a G&T and some toasted cashew nuts for the best part of the first hour. She's feeling quite pensive this evening, full of gratitude for the people she has met in her life, particularly 'the boyz' in Cape Town. Four different personalities, different countries, and four hearts of gold. She has grown particularly fond of Ivan, perhaps because of his innocence, his greenness. He is not worldly wise and still finds joy in such simple pleasures. Is it because she was the same, or wants to be again?

-§-

They're in quite a hurry, walking briskly down Kloof Street enroute to their hotel to meet a repeat guest from France, who apparently needed to meet the owners this afternoon. The two of them race past Serge's. Maybe she would manage a quick wave to Marie, but she is busy behind the bar and only catches a glimpse of them as they are almost out of sight. They continue walking, with William on the road side of the footpath. *Such a gentleman*, Annie thinks. Suddenly, and quite unexpectedly, Marie is running behind them calling to them. 'Bill, Annie, wait a minute.'

'Hi Marie,' Annie says. 'We are in a bit of a rush, we have a meeting in 15 minutes.'

'Sorry to stop you. It's just that you really have to meet these two guys who are new in Cape Town. They're having lunch at Serge's and I have told them about you several times, and they are very keen to meet you. They have just finished renovating a beautiful guesthouse in Upper Gardens. Really nice guys.' She smiles pleadingly, mostly at William, Annie notes.

'Well, we have a few minutes to say hi,' William says. Annie stares at him in disbelief.

They walk back up the street a few metres to the alcove on the right of the entrance of Serge's, Annie's favorite spot in the restaurant.

'Ivan and Kris, may I introduce you to Annie and William.' Marie says, standing on the footpath next to them. She looks satisfied with her mission and heads back to the bar.

'Hi, I'm Kris and this is Ivan, just to clear that up,' Kris says with a smile, extending his hand and standing to formally meet them both. 'I dare say it's somewhat easier working out who is who with the two of you,' he adds.

Annie smiles and allows William to continue chatting with Kris. She turns to Ivan, the less confident of the two of them. He is a handsome man with grey hair and a bright face. He is not big in stature, but he has a presence. Annie looks at his face and notices his clear green eyes, 'What beautiful eyes you have.'

'All the better to see you with,' Ivan replies with a wolfish smile.

Annie smiles at the joke, 'I'm terribly sorry we can't stay long. We have a meeting in a few minutes. But I'm very certain we will have many occasions in the future to get to know you both. We are only occasionally in Cape Town; we mostly live in London.'

'Wow! That sounds like a great lifestyle. I've only been to London twice. The first time was about twenty-five years ago. Such a beautiful city.'

'What were you? Five years old back then?' Annie winks.

Ivan smiles, 'Kettle, pot, black!'

Annie laughs.

'We have been here in Cape Town only a few months, and we love it. We have a small guesthouse in Gardens,' Ivan says.

'So I hear, and recently renovated. Marie is the font of all knowledge here; if Marie doesn't know you, then you're not worth knowing.'

'Then it's a relief she knows us.'

'Oh, who wouldn't notice the two of you? You will get on very well here.' Annie looks at her watch, 'We really must keep moving, Bill. So sorry to have to rush off. We have an appointment at the hotel.' She slides her arm around the back of William's waist. 'But listen, why don't the two of you swing by the house sometime and we can open a bottle and get to know you some more. We have the boutique hotel on Upper Union Street. Pop in there and they can direct you to the house. We will let them know. It's Ivan and…'

'Kris,' Kris says.

'Perfect,' Annie confirms, smiling at Ivan.

'Better still,' William adds, 'if you're free Sunday, why not come over for a braai? We'll get some others over as well. Perhaps Ayden and Daniel are free. Do you know them?'

'Yes, we have met. Sounds like a plan,' Kris says.

William rushes inside the restaurant to scribble details down on a piece of paper. Annie watches Kris and Ivan staring helplessly at William, striding masculinely into the restaurant. She looks at Marie who, of course, is blushing and a little weak at the knees. *My sexy husband.*

He returns, handing the note to Kris. 'Say, around 1pm?'

'Perfect,' Kris replies, taking the note.

'Please don't bring anything,' Annie says, 'We have plenty.' She turns to William, 'We have to go, BB.' Turning to head down the street, she winks at Ivan, 'See you on Sunday.'

'They seem like nice lads,' William says as they begin to jog down the street.

'Very nice,' Annie concurs.

-§-

They clear immigration and customs without concern, and walk out of the door into the delightfully warm morning air. Annie breathes it in and smiles. Whatever Cape Town lacks in sophistication, it makes up for with the weather, and that feeling that you're not cooped up.

A car is waiting for them. The driver jumps out and over-enthusiastically grabs their luggage and almost comically shoves it in the car boot. William opens the door for Annie. 'Welcome back to Cape Town,' she says with a smile to William. Settling into the seat behind the driver, she feigns assiduity on her phone, politely ignoring the initiated, inane conversation from the driver.

'To the house first,' William instructs as he climbs into the seat next to Annie. He reaches over and feels her knee, and slides his hand slightly up her thigh. She looks into his eyes, and they smile. There is a lugubrious look in William's eyes, and she puts her hand on his and squeezes it tightly.

'I'll organise lunch with Ayden and Daniel,' William says, reaching for his phone. It had become a tradition for the four of them to have lunch on the day they arrived in Cape Town.

'I'm interested in the story about Marie. Maybe we should have lunch at Manna Epicure,' Annie says.

'Good idea.'

'Let's hope that intolerable waiter is not working the lunch shift. He should have lost his job after the debacle with my salmon last time we went there.'

William smiles, 'It was a debacle, for sure.'

Annie smiles and starts to laugh nervously out loud, a little embarrassed, knowing it was she who really caused the fiasco, and allowed it to get out of hand, once she recognised the waiter was her weaker adversary. She looks again at William and sees a tear falling down his cheek. 'You OK?'

William turns to her and smiles, 'I love you. I hope you know that. I always have and always will.'

-§-

A couple of years before meeting William, Annie was fortunately in the right place at the right time in Dublin, to get a promotion, based in Medina. She was working for an airline company at the time, which most of her friends thought was a ruse, because she always seemed to be 'conveniently' invited to the soirées of sheiks and influential businessmen. She's known by her closest friends as 007, and she loves being perceived as a little mysterious.

She is fit and, accordingly in the UAE, has little opportunity to drink alcohol, so at times she feels invincible. That is until she catches the eye of an extremely sexy man in the middle of the desert. It's literally love at first sight, but she is intent on trying to play hard-to-get, at least for a couple of weeks. Her friends tell the real story though; given the onslaught of flowers, romantic and sensual texts, and sweet gifts, she caved in within a few days. William not only looks magnificent - toned and well-proportioned, wavy blonde hair, and dark skin - but his flashy smile and piercing eyes make Annie melt every time she sees him. The coup de grâce is that he is utterly charming - gentlemanly, confident, caring, funny, just perfect. The two become inseparable, and it is evident to all their friends that their love is strong and real. So when William tells Annie that he is finishing in Medina and is going back to London, Annie quits her job to be with the man she has fallen in love with.

-§-

After unpacking, resetting their kitchen, and retrieving their personal effects which are in storage during their time in London, Annie takes a refreshing shower. She loves being back in Cape Town, and in their spacious home. William joins her in the shower, sliding his hands around her waist, and kisses the side of her neck. After all these years, she still enjoys the feel of William. His hands, his arms, his lips, his chest rubbing against her back.

'We don't want to be late for lunch,' Annie suggests.

'Are you sure?'

'Well just a little late, then.' She swings around, and runs her hands down his chest.

'I'm opting for a lot late.' He grins and pulls her close to him.

William and Annie stroll up Kloof Street toward the mountain and saunter into Manna Epicure. Ayden and Daniel are already there and have started on a bottle of sauvignon blanc. There is a petite silver ice bucket with tongs on the table. Annie looks at Ayden and smiles. *He knows me so well.*

'You two are late,' Daniel declares, jumping up to give them both a big hug. Ayden winks at Annie knowingly. 'Nice to see you both again. How was the flight? You look radiant, Annie.'

The four friends settle into a wonderful afternoon of food, wine, and catching up on all the news on both sides of the globe.

'So, tell me about Marie,' Annie says.

Daniel starts. 'Everything started normally, we were having lunch with Kris and Ivan. Then she saw someone across the street from her restaurant and started staggering and chanting, like she was possessed, 'no, no, no', she was saying.'

'Then she passed out. Completely out cold,' Ayden takes over. 'She dropped the bottle. It smashed everywhere, and she literally collapsed. Ivan and I were trying to check that she was still alive. I called an ambulance, which only took a few minutes to get there, and they carted her off to the Mediclinic Hospital.'

'Extreme shock,' Daniel says. 'Brought on by post-traumatic stress, apparently.'

'Shit,' William says, 'Is she OK now?'

'Well,' Ayden says, 'you know Marie. She is basically in denial about it all. She claims it was mistaken identity, remembering her friend with an abusive uncle who looked like this guy she saw in the street.'

'It's a bit of a weird weird story, if you ask me,' Daniel states. 'What's more weird, however, is - and I forgot to tell you this as well, Ayden - I saw the guy sprinting away after Marie fainted. I'm sure I have seen him on a couple of occasions before, around town. AND, Kris said he recognised him as well, and that he came into the gallery once and bought a small sculpture by Stas. Kris said he was from Paris.'

'It's a village here, right?' Annie adds, trying to make sense of it all.

'What does he look like?' William asks curiously.

'Good-looking guy. Clearly Mediterranean, you know, olive skin, dark hair, but greying a bit. Tall, and, on the few occasions I've seen him, seems to be well-dressed. Again, classic European,' Daniel describes.

'Sounds like the French gentleman staying at the hotel,' Annie says with some intrigue. 'Is he still staying there, BB? Perhaps you should have a word with him.'

'He checked out yesterday, according to the manager in our conversation this morning. Paid in cash as always,' William says. He looks at Ayden, who is unusually pensive, and suddenly pale and concerned looking. 'You're very quiet. What's the matter?'

'Mmm, miles away. I need to get some things from the supermarket before we head back to the guesthouse. I'll go and see how Marie is getting on this afternoon.' Speaking quickly, Ayden forces a smile on his face. Annie recognises that look. Undoubtedly he knows more about the situation than he is letting on. She knows Ayden is tremendously loyal to people; if he promised to keep a secret, he would take it to his grave.

Ayden gets up from the table. 'Shall we get the bill?'

Ivan

How the fuck did I get here? Ivan asks himself as he settles into his comfortable, but still newish, leather couch. Glass of red wine in hand, after packing a few boxes of personal effects. He overthinks his question, debating whether it's rhetorical or not. He knows the answer, of course, but he enjoys the process of thought. Moreover he enjoys (over)analysing the journey he has made. One of the many lessons he learned from the Jesuits in the school where he worked in Adelaide, was that in order to move forward, you must understand from where you have come. Long before he started working with the Jesuits, however, even as a boy in Whyalla, where he grew up, Ivan had worked on mastering the craft of overthinking. He inherited the skill from his grandfather, who was also a master of worrying, which ultimately caused his death. Ivan was also in the early stages of mastering the same 'art'.

Tomorrow the removal company will pick up the boxes. His furniture will be taken by a young, starry-eyed British expat the day after, and on Saturday Ivan will again 'move forward', flying out to be with Kris in Berlin, then, together, to Cape Town. He holds his glass up as if to toast the situation: his final days after two years of work and fun in Hong Kong. The first two years of his new life, and the city where he met the love of his life.

He takes a sip of wine. It's certainly too hot and humid in Hong Kong in June to drink red wine, but some old habits die hard, *and that's why we have air con.* He thinks back over the past years and smiles. *It's been a hell of a journey so far.* After the rather traumatic experience of coming out to his wife of nineteen years, to his family, his friends, and his work colleagues, he was unsure how to reconcile his old life with the new gay Ivan. However, as if the universe aligned at exactly the right moment, a position became available in Hong Kong, which seemed, to Ivan, to be the perfect opportunity for starting again, leaving home and country.

The Lufthansa flight arrives in Cape Town ridiculously early in the morning. After clearing immigration and collecting their significant amount of luggage, they catch a taxi to the Lady Victoria Bed and Breakfast. Kris and Ivan had purchased the seriously dilapidated, but beautiful, Victorian homestead whilst on holiday together less than six months ago, with a vision to starting a new guesthouse. Effectively this is the start of a completely new life for them both. Ivan stares out of the taxi window, a little in disbelief, and a little excited. It is still dark, and the expanse of weak street lights in Khayelitsha lay testament to the glaring inequality in post-apartheid South Africa.

As they arrive at the b'n'b, the manager meets them at the door and greets them warmly, but professionally. It is still very early and no other staff are in the house. It is cold in the house. *That will need to change*, Ivan thinks. They are shown to the largest room, and they decide to jump into bed; it's too early to do anything else.

Later that morning, Ivan and Kris meet the other staff, gathered in the living room, and start by advising them that they will all be staying on. Ivan senses their relief.

'There will be some major renovations made to the house, and necessarily, you will all need new uniforms, and the way we serve, clean, and work in the house will have to change,' Kris announces to the staff, who all look somewhat shell-shocked.

'We will be helping you make the changes with some training, so there is no need to be concerned,' Ivan adds, trying to allay their fears.

Within four weeks Ivan and Kris had started the renovations on the tired house. The new guesthouse branding, website, uniforms, and everything else, were well underway. Kris and Ivan managed to get away from the chaos regularly, whether sharing a bottle of wine on the Promenade at Camps Bay, or lunch, with wine, at their new favorite restaurant on Kloof Street. Ivan is enjoying his new life. 'This is sooo far removed from working as a teacher in Australia, or Hong Kong for that matter,' he says coming into Serge's, as he looks out into the street, catching a small glimpse of Table

Mountain behind some new, god-awful-looking apartments across the street.

'Yeah, do you like it?' Kris asks.

'I've never lived or worked like this before. You know, when you can create your own agenda and time schedule. I'm liking it very much. I've never had wine for lunch during the working week in all my life. So, thank you for saving me from a life of drudgery.' Ivan smiles, and squeezes Kris's shoulder. 'Cheers, buddy. I love you.'

Ivan's body shudders with excitement, and he smiles inwardly. He loves Kris like he has never loved a human being before. Even during the nineteen years of marriage to his wife, he didn't realise being in love really felt like this. Now in his early 40s, he is as giddy as a child, having been spun around on a playground spinner. *Life is full and grand*, he thinks.

After confirming that Pierre is not working this afternoon, they settle into their usual space near the kitchen where there are two power outlets for their laptops, to continue work on their website and 'stuff'. Marie serves them and chats a little bit with Kris in some foreign gibberish.

Marie walks off to arrange their order, and Kris and Ivan, so caught up with their work, don't notice two guys walk into the restaurant. Ivan only notices them when Kris gets up to go and talk with them. Marie is there as well, so Ivan, not being overly confident, decides to continue working on his laptop. Kris comes back some time later. 'Nice guys, from the UK. Ayden and, umm, Daniel, I believe. They also own a guesthouse - something Manor. Live in Kensington or something. We must make sure we remember that so we can invite them to the opening.'

'Should I check with them to get it right?' Ivan inquires.

'Nah, our manager will know.'

Sometime later, Ayden and Daniel walk up to Ivan and Kris and introduce themselves to Ivan. Good looking guys, Ivan thinks. Ayden is clearly the leader of the pack. Daniel is physically stronger, but to some extent more scruffy; Ivan just wants to tuck his shirt in properly for him. He has fantastic brown hair, which could do with a proper cut and style, and a pleasant looking face, with far-away eyes, that seem to be focused somewhere else.

'We're on our way back to the grindstone,' Ayden jests. 'Lovely to meet you both, and I'm sure we will see more of you again. It's a village here.'

Renovations to the house are finished, and the new Victoria Boutique Villa will be open for business in just a week. There are even the first guests booked, so Kris and Ivan make plans to have a party to celebrate. Ivan assists their manager to compile a guest list, ensuring that Kensington Manor is included. However, on the day of the party, Ivan checks the responses to the invitation and can't see Ayden or Daniel on the list. It is then that he realises their guesthouse was not invited. 'This is one Kris can sort out himself. What a fuck-up,' Ivan mumbles to himself as he leaves the living room.

It is a beautiful evening - cool, clear and no wind, a definite bonus. Guests arrive and Ivan and Kris initially start together as a couple welcoming people and introducing themselves. After a short time they're separately entertaining neighbours and guests, showing people around the house and the various aspects of the renovation. Ivan, in the front garden, chatting with their Italian neighbours from across the road, is interrupted by Kris, 'Excuse me, Ivan, there is someone you have to meet. Sorry to interrupt.' He leads Ivan up the stairs and into the living room. 'Rachel, this is Ivan. Rachel owns and operates Freedom House, practically around the corner from us,' Kris says and excuses himself to mingle with other guests.

'There are a number of guesthouses in this area. Must be the right suburb to be in, right?' Ivan says.

'That's exactly what Kris said to me. Have you guys been rehearsing some opening lines?' she laughs.

Ivan smiles, 'Perhaps we should have shared with each other our opening lines before this evening.'

Rachel smiles. 'And just so you know, I think you're officially in Upper Gardens, not Tamboerskloof.'

'Ahh, the second talking point from Kris,' Ivan says with a smile. 'You see, we did try a few lines out on each other. Let's get some more champagne.'

'Where are you actually from, Ivan? I can't pick the accent.'
'Originally from Adelaide, South Australia, but let's say I tried very hard to disguise my accent for many years. So now it's just a bizarre Australian blend.'
'Ahh, I hear it now,' Rachel says with a smile. 'I'm clearly from the UK.'
'Clearly! Tell me, you've been here for a few years now, and we have just arrived. What do you miss most from the UK?'
Rachel runs her hand over her mouth as she thinks, but Ivan notices more to wipe drops of champagne falling out. 'Hmm, I guess it would be good theatre, and the galleries. I mean, there are some plays and musicals put on here, but I miss the West End.'
'OK, I imagine. I used to work a lot in musical theatre in Adelaide and in Hong Kong. It would be great to get back into it, or at least see a few shows here.'
'That's fantastic, wow! I love going to see shows here. It's not the West End, but it will do for me. To be honest, I find it difficult to find people to go with. I have made quite a few friends here, sometimes by accident,' she giggles. 'But too few people want to go and see musicals with me.' She looks at Ivan, 'Well, at last I have a theatre buddy.' she declares. They clink their glasses.
'Listen,' Ivan continues, 'there is a production of 'Chess' playing at a small theatre in Camps Bay.'
'Theatre on the Bay,' Rachel says.
'Yeah, that's it. It's on next week. I'm very curious to see how they do it, in such a small venue, with very little space for a large set, and a big company, I'm guessing, and where do you put the musicians? I mean, the score is huge. Would you like to come with me? Kris is not one for musicals.'
'That sounds wonderful. I don't know it at all.'
'One of my favourites. I think the music is wonderful. Book by Tim Rice and the music and lyrics by Benny and Björn - you know - the boys from ABBA.'
'It's a date. How exciting, we're off to see a musical together already.' Rachel says, looking a little stupefied.

Ivan smiles warmly at Rachel, not entirely sure she has taken it all in. In any case, he gets to go and see his favorite show with someone. He gestures to the staff for another top-up and, through the bay window, sees Marie on the veranda talking to Kris. 'Come, let's meet some others,' he says to Rachel and leads her to the veranda, 'Rachel, can I introduce you to Marie.'

'Marie!' Rachel says with surprise. 'We know each other. It's a village here.'

'Then I don't need to tell you that Marie owns one of the best restaurants in Cape Town.' Ivan declares. 'But Marie, darling, and this may be the champagne talking, you have to do something with Pierre! He is no asset to your restaurant.' Unable to stop himself saying more, he adds, 'We are in the habit now of driving by to see if he is there before we decide whether to come in.'

'Oh my word, that was you the other day, in the Jeep,' Rachel says.

'Could well have been.'

Marie smiles wryly, 'In due course.'

Such a beautiful evening, Ivan thinks. He looks out into the street and catches a glimpse of a tall figure lurking in the shadows of a tree on Bath Street. *Who the fuck is that?,* he thinks. Turning back to his guests, 'Who's for a top-up?' He looks out to the street again, but the figure has gone. *Fucking weird, creepy.* He performs a dramatic pirouette and heads into the living room to get a bottle of champagne.

Ivan parks the Jeep in front of Freedom House and jumps out to ring the bell, but Rachel is already at the door. She has donned a colourful, tight, short-sleeved dress, with a beautiful auburn shawl which matches her hair, and block heeled black shoes. 'You look nice,' Ivan says, then rethinks, and regrets the comment, *Nice?! What a terrible word to use.* Then he starts singing in his mind a line from 'Into The Woods', *You're not good, You're not bad, You're just nice!*

'Thank you, just a little something from the old world.'

'Ready to go? I'm pretty excited to see this show again. Last time I saw 'Chess' was in Melbourne. That would have been in… fuck, no idea. Something from my old world,' Ivan says with a wink.

They set off, turning left onto Kloof Nek Road heading toward Table Mountain. It's a beautiful night, if not a little chilly. Rachel is chatting, and Ivan confirms her chit-chat every now and then with a smile and a nod. He continues to muse over his stupid 'nice' comment. *I have a fuckin' Masters in Education, and the best I can do is 'nice'… and, what kind of bogan would string together 'fuckin'' and 'Masters in Education', and why are you still using the term bogan?* He starts playing with the sound of the word 'nice', employing his best Australian accent. *Noice. Youz look real noice.* The Australian TV show 'Kath and Kim' comes to mind, and he laughs out loud.

'I know, right. It's just too funny. I mean, how is that possible?' Rachel says. Then there's silence.

Ivan turns left on the Promenade at Camps Bay. Rachel points to the car park opposite the theatre. 'If you can find a park in the car park, grab it.'

'Sounds like a plan,' Ivan says in disbelief.

They stroll into the theatre foyer, 'It's even smaller than I thought,' Ivan says.

'It's very charming, but you're right, very small. Almost like a cute community theatre in Brighton.'

'Is that where you came from, Brighton?'

'Yes, that's a few years ago now, another life.'

The theatre bells ring, and, almost in a manner 'Pavlovian', punters scramble to get to their seats.

'Here we go, first stop 'Merano'.'

-§-

It was in the Whyalla Institute, 1975, when Ivan first saw a live musical production, albeit the 'Whyalla Players' amateur production of 'The Sound of Music'. He was in awe. The singing, the lights, the costumes, the fake scenery, the music, the smell of the floor boards; it was a night he will never forget. He had to stand against the side wall in order to see the show as some inconsiderate woman, sitting directly in front of him, on a flat floor, decided to continue wearing her enormous hat throughout the show. Ivan's mum was too caught up in the show to ask, and his sisters certainly didn't want to change seats.

He went to bed singing 'Cloim ev'ry Moun'in', and wondering if there really was a way to solve a problem like Maria, or whether it was just her friends who really didn't understand her, and in fact, there was no problem. And wondering what 'dough-a-deer' really meant, perhaps a new recipe, and what was it that Maria couldn't face?

His sisters could only remark on how long it was, how hard the seats were, and how hot it was, but for Ivan… he could not forget that face, that smile, that young man on stage, how striking he looked, how handsome, 'Going on seventeen'.

-§-

'What did you think?' Rachel asks, bringing two glasses of sparkling wine to their table in the foyer.

'Well, I must say, on the whole, it was creative staging, but the most disappointing aspect was the use of a backing track in lieu of real musicians, and then, the delirium of having a 'conductor' is bewildering. It's the first time I've seen a 'professional' musical with a conductor, conducting a backing track.'

'Can I be honest? I have no idea what you're talking about.'

They laugh, and clink their glasses.

'Tell me,' Ivan says, 'you mentioned Brighton earlier. Too early to share? Or… is there a story there?'

'I'll tell you mine, if you tell me yours,' Rachel says with a smile. 'I lived for many years in Brighton and I owned a tea shop, together with my husband. After he died, I sold up and moved to Cape Town. A new life for me.'

'Very succinct,' Ivan says, 'which will make my story all the more laborious.' He takes a long swig of bubbles, then breathes. 'Born and raised in Whyalla, South Australia, got married, way too young, to a good Christian girl. Fast forward nineteen years, divorced after I came out, and moved to Hong Kong, and met Kris... Tada! Here we are! Indeed a new life for me too.'

'You see, you can do succinct! But I'm guessing there are some painful nuances missing from the story. Well done you for being true to yourself.'

'Albeit later in life.'

'But then, you may never have met Kris.'

'True.'

'The stars align. Here's to life's unexpected turns, and living each day.' They clink glasses.

-§-

On his knees next to his bed, Ivan prays for clarity, with humility and sincerity. 'I'm not sure getting married is the best way forward. I have doubts and serious 'alternative' feelings... She's a very beautiful girl, and I love her, and really enjoy being with her... Will that be enough?.. But what about the way I feel? You know... that way.' He looks up, almost looking for a sign, then closes his eyes again. A tear rolls down his cheek as he reminds himself of the Church's rhetoric, and the Bible, but moreover, of the comments, thoughts, and fervent dogmatic opinions of his parents and close friends. 'I'm gonna need Your help, every day, but Your will be done.'

-§-

In the passenger seat of the car, heading toward Serge's, Ivan smiles as he reminisces, *The first time I was on my knees next to my bed in Hong Kong wasn't for prayer.* 'Slow down,' he says to Kris as they front the restaurant. 'I can't see him. Oh wait... there's Marie. It's safe to go in.'

Kris parks the Jeep partly on the footpath right in front of the 'No Parking' sign, as always. They both jump out and saunter into the restaurant, sitting in their new favourite spot, the alcove next to the bar. Marie comes over and gives them each a hug and three kisses. Kris orders a glass of sauvignon blanc and a chopped salad with beef, and Ivan, his head elsewhere, orders the same.

'Bookings are good,' Ivan says.

'Mmm. I think we need to find a new manager. I'm not entirely happy with the way she is operating the guesthouse. The only 'value added' is that she takes calls and bookings at home after hours. But for the rest, she seems overly controlling, and she is very derogatory to the staff. I don't like it.'

'Right.' Ivan responds as he watches Marie race out of the restaurant as if there were a fire. She returns a minute later with a very attractive couple.

'Ivan and Kris, may I introduce you to Annie and William.' Marie says, still standing on the footpath.

Oh my god, he's fuckin' fit, Ivan thinks.

'Hi, I'm Kris and this is Ivan, just to clear that up,' Kris says, smiling, as he stands and shakes their hands. 'I dare say it's somewhat easier working out who is who with the two of you.'

My witty man, Ivan thinks, in his intoxicated adoration of the couple. William is an incredibly good-looking man - fit, proportionately muscular with the classic 'v' shape. Beautiful skin, wavy sun-bleached hair that you just want to run your fingers through, bright blue eyes, and a 'fuck-me' smile that's enough to make you 'stand to attention'. Annie is classically beautiful - slim, fit, beautifully dressed, and, as if in an advert, her fine, straight blonde hair dances in the light breeze and catches the sunlight. She flicks it out of her face as she looks to Ivan. 'What beautiful eyes you have.'

Completely caught off guard that she could be interested in him, he replies 'All the better to see you with.' He smiles, a little embarrassed, thinking that was one of the dimmest responses he has come up with.

Annie smiles at the joke, 'I'm terribly sorry we can't stay long. We have a meeting in a few minutes. But I'm very certain we will have many occasions in the future to get to know you both. We are only occasionally in Cape Town; we mostly live in London.'

'Wow! That sounds like a great lifestyle. I've only been to London twice. The first time was about twenty-five years ago. Such a beautiful city.' *God, I can babble...*

'What were you? Five years old back then?' Annie winks.

Ivan smiles. *Yes, I was very young, but look at you two!* 'Kettle, pot, black!' Annie laughs.

'We have been here in Cape Town only a few months, and we love it. We have a small guesthouse in Gardens,' Ivan says, trying to get the conversation back on track.

'So I hear, and recently renovated. Marie is the font of all knowledge here; if Marie doesn't know you, then you're not worth knowing.'

'Then it's a relief she knows us,' he says with complete sincerity.

'Oh, who wouldn't notice the two of you? You will get on very well here.'

Ivan swoons. *What a lovely thing to say.*

'We really must keep moving, Bill. So sorry to have to rush off. We have an appointment at the hotel.' She slides her arm around the back of William's waist, and Ivan has a ping of something inside him. He can't discern between being jealous of Annie, feeling such a body, or jealous of William having such a body. *What must it be like to have such a body - either way?*, Ivan briefly dreams, then returns to reality. 'We have the boutique hotel on Upper Union Street,' Annie says. 'Pop in there and they can direct you to the house. We will let them know. It's Ivan and...'

'Kris' Kris says.

'Perfect,' Annie confirms, smiling at Ivan, who is still in a bit of a daze.

'Better still,' William adds, 'If you're free Sunday, why not come over for a braai? We'll get some others over as well. Perhaps Ayden and Daniel are free. Do you know them?'

'Yes, we have met. Sounds like a plan,' Kris says.

William strides inside the restaurant. Ivan can't help but stare at the grace, beauty, and agility of William's movement as he playfully capers up to the bar. He catches a glimpse of Marie, who is clearly besotted. *Not the only one then.*

He returns, handing a piece of paper to Kris. 'Say around 1pm?'

'Perfect,' Kris replies, taking the note.

'Please don't bring anything,' Annie says in a manner like clicking her fingers to bring Ivan back to reality, 'We have plenty. We have to go, BB.'

Annie gently leads her beautiful man down the street and turns her head to wink at Ivan, as if to say *He's mine*, 'See you on Sunday.'

'He's a fit bunny.' Ivan says, verbalising what he imagines Kris is also thinking.

'Nice couple,' Kris replies. 'What do you think 'BB' stands for?'

Best Butt, Buff Bod, Beguiling Biceps. 'Big Bucks?' Ivan suggests, with a big smile.

-§-

It was so incredibly liberating to be able to enjoy and express all, well most, of the thoughts Ivan had bottled up over so many years. As an adolescent, a young man, and a married man for several years, still hiding his feelings and thoughts from his family and friends. Even as a musical director of amateur musical theatre, surrounded by strong, confident gay guys, Ivan felt unable to be himself. The 'pleasant day(s) out' with his closest work colleagues, after too many beers, sitting in a bar listening to his mate's rendition of 'Nobody Knows the Trouble I've Seen', Ivan, ironically, still kept his feelings under wraps. Ultimately it all started to fall apart, and he was losing grip on his control, giving way to freeing himself, albeit slowly and clumsily.

In hindsight, Ivan knows he should have spent more energy on bravely coming out when he was young, and less on hiding the truth. After so many years of controlling himself, he let go of the reins, and callously continued riding a completely out-of-control horse, heading for a cliff.

-§-

Annie links Ivan's arm and whisks him away, just as he starts to stare at the lady in the fancy dress costume, 'Let me show you around the house' she says.

'That's some outfit, eh? Here was I worried about what to wear.'

Annie smiles.

'This place is enormous. Just the two of you here? You must feel like you're rattling around a lot.'

'Well, we really only use a few rooms in the front, so this back part hardly ever gets used unless we have guests.'

'It's quite spectacular. Beautiful details, and so much space. It's like travelling first class. I did that once on Emirates to Australia, got an upgrade. I was completely shell-shocked, couldn't make a decision about anything. I'm a bit used to being told when to eat. Let's say I settled into it after an hour.' Ivan winks to Annie.

'I'm sure you did,' Annie says as she squeezes his arm. 'Let's get back to the party.'

Arriving back in the garden, Ivan picks up his red wine. 'Your house is spectacular, spacious, and so beautifully decorated,' he says to William.

Ivan sees Daniel and nods. He and Annie head over to Ayden, who is chatting with the curiously attired lady. He enthusiastically shakes Ivan's hand and grabs his upper arm with his other hand. Ayden turns to Annie and gives her a kiss on her cheek. 'Lovely to see you both again,' Ayden says, 'Can I introduce you to Marge? She's a friend of Rachel's, visiting for a month from the UK.'

William approaches Ayden. 'Can I borrow you for a moment? I need some advice in the kitchen.' Ayden follows William into the kitchen through the beautiful French doors of the dining room.

'I really like what you're wearing,' Ivan says to Marge. 'It's very unique.'

Annie spills a little of her wine, and needs to go inside to get a cloth.

-§-

Kris steers the Jeep onto Camps Bay Drive toward the mountain. Ivan looks over to him. 'It was a good send-off, don't you think? Appropriate.'

'Yeah, still can't believe she's gone.'

'I know. It's a little bit sad that we, her friends, had to make the arrangements for her funeral. No family present, not even Pierre. Weird!'

'I, mercifully, haven't seen Pierre for some time now. Actually, I'm glad he was not involved, adding a level of awkwardness to the evening. It was important for us all to say goodbye, in our own way, but together.'

'We're really going to miss her. Don't mean to be dark, but I find it a bit ironic that we had her cremated, given the fire destroyed everything beyond recognition. I mean what was there to cremate?'

'It's probably the way she wanted it to be. You know she never did things by half. Even her chips were cooked three times.'

They look at each other and smile. A tear rolls down Ivan's face, and Kris reaches out to squeeze his leg.

'Rachel told me the police found the diamond from her ring. The only thing still recognisable.'

'I'm surprised one of the police didn't steal it.'

The Incident

'I tell you, I've seen him. He's here in Cape Town. I saw him today.'

'OK, OK, I'll make some arrangements and see what flights are available for tomorrow. You can stay here if you need to.'

'God only knows how long he's been here. It could have been weeks, years even.'

'Listen, you have to calm down a little bit. Stay alert, but please calm down.'

'OK, OK…'

'I have to go now, but call me if you feel that something, anything, develops. Right?'

'Aha.'

'Right?.. Call me.'

'Yes, OK.' Pierre finishes his call and stands in the dark room for a few moments with his hands by his side, numb. Eventually the glow of his phone abates, and the room plunges into total darkness. He has to step up to the plate. He's so tired of pretending to be the foolish, absent-minded, autistiform brother. It was he who had masterminded Marie's escape in Lille but now he is genuinely petrified for his life and for Marie's. He has to act, *but how?*

He looks out of the window of his tiny apartment in Hout Bay, but he can't see anything. He shivers as he looks into the blackness. It's an atypical moonless autumn night - dark, cold, and the dampness is close, like waking up between sodden sheets of cold sweat. It's ridiculously cold in his apartment, clearly built for the summer tourists, without any consideration to heating for the colder months. Brick walls, plaster, no insulation, and single glazed windows in tired wooden frames.

A car's headlights cast a sliver of light on Pierre's face, illuminating his furrowed forehead for a second. He collects his thoughts, *I'll have to drive to Cape Town to see if she's OK.* It's at least a 30 minute drive from Hout

Bay, and if the traffic is bad, it could take longer. He grabs his car keys and his black sweater, and heads out the door.

It's so fockin' cold, Marie thinks as she grabs her car keys and heads out the door. At least it's not raining. She is a bit late to relieve the staff at the end of evening service, after taking a call from Ayden, who is again concerned about the mental health of Pierre. *If only Ayden knew his real character.* Pierre had, in fact, concocted the whole idea and plan, and encouraged Marie to leave Lucien. He organised the flight, the escape route, and the distraction for Lucien in order for Marie to slip out through the fire escape, strangely enough, on a night not dissimilar to this one. Marie had, of course, told Pierre that she confided in Ayden about her previous life in Lille. Pierre was not happy about that, but ultimately conceded that Marie needed to be honest with a few close friends.

She could have made it to the restaurant in time, but somehow the concept of 'mobile' phone eludes her. Preferring to chat in one place, in the privacy of her apartment, rather than being 'mobile' and chatting, which she always finds rather vulgar and egocentric. Moreover she has come to feel the need to stay alert in all public areas, and a 'mobile' phone call is clearly a distraction.

She jumps into her car, locks the doors, and immediately starts the engine. Then, and only then, she feels she has the time and security to arrange her handbag, scarf, and coat. She imagines, because it's so cold, there will not be anyone in the restaurant, a bit like lunch service today. *I hope they've kept the fire alight.*

Marie, necessarily, had had the chimney cleaned after it caught light during evening service last year. It caused quite a scene, and the patrons were initially panicked and annoyed, but later, on the whole, they embraced the drama and a few were delighted to chat to the local TV crew covering the event, talking about 'the horror' and 'escaping just before the flames lapped at their table'. Marie smiles remembering the young attractive firefighter with whom she exchanged numbers, and who later came to visit her at her apartment, to 'check if she was OK'. She starts to hum strains of 'Come on baby, light my fire.'

You have to love this cold weather, Rachel thinks to herself as she dresses to go out for the evening with her friends. 'Then you can reeealllly dress up,' she sings as an operatic aria, adjusting her slacks. She has been through a number of outfits, and they lay on her bed, rejected. 'How do you solve a problem like my dresses,' she sings as she puts her beautiful black heels back in their box, *too good for tonight*, and opts for a pair of sparkling grey slippers. It has always been comfort over fashion for Rachel. She looks at herself in the freestanding mirror next to her bed, wearing new dark grey slacks with a high waist and an exaggeratedly large shiny belt, with a black woolen cardigan speckled with shiny gold thread, over a white blouse. 'Perfect,' she says out loud. Her phone pings; a message to confirm the Uber driver is waiting outside. *He's quite a bit early,* Rachel thinks as she grabs her handbag, her scarf, and coat and races out the door, so as to not inconvenience the driver waiting for her. She jumps in the back seat. 'The Artscape, please. Oh, you probably already know that, right?' She giggles a little as the car drives off.

'I can't remember it being this cold in March,' Kris sings out from the shower to Ivan. He stands for a moment and allows the water to warm him up. 'I still can't believe you bought me a ticket for tonight. I'll need a few drinks before I can sit through this show, I can tell you that for free.' He turns off the taps and steps out into the cold bathroom. *'Jezus,* it's cold.' He grabs the white towel from the rail and dries his hair first, then his face and body. After wiping the mirror, fogged with steam, he wraps the towel around his waist, and looks at himself in the mirror. *Not bad, for an old guy,* he thinks.
Ivan comes into the bathroom partially dressed. 'You'll love it. Who can't resist a good song and dance show?'

'What are you wearing… on top I mean.'

'I'm gonna go for a white shirt and a black jacket.'

'You'll need more than that, I'm guessing.'

'It'll be warm in the theatre, so it's just cold between cars and buildings.'

'OK, don't say I didn't warn you. I'm gonna wear a sweater and a jacket, and a scarf. What's this sing-a-long called again?'

Ivan plants a kiss on Kris's cheek and pulls the towel from off his waist. 'The Sound of Music,' he throws the towel at him, 'and you'll love it,' he says as he leaves the bathroom.

'Is that an instruction or a prediction?'

'It's an unusually cold night here tonight, so please take an extra sweater or scarf if you have one. It's not normally like this in late March.' Ayden instructs his guests as they leave for the evening. 'I've made the booking at Serge's under your name. I'm confident you'll enjoy your supper.'

Ayden closes the front door after his guests are safely in their taxi. The last guests to leave for the evening, and now he has time to deal with other issues. *I'd better call Marie first,* Ayden thinks. He had, some minutes ago, received a call from Pierre, who was his usual dismantled self - excessively panic stricken and a little delirious. In any case, Marie should be warned that he is in a state.

He can hear the phone ringing on the other end, as he stares into the backyard of the guesthouse, noticing some items from guests left by the pool. *When did I become a mother to these feckin' people?* 'Hiya, it's just me.'

'Hi, Ayden. Let me guess, it's about Pierre. He tried calling me earlier, but I couldn't be arsed listening to it again. Like a broken record.'

'Does anyone say 'record' anymore?' He laughs. 'Are you sure he's OK? He sounded pretty upset this time. I tried to calm him down but I'm not sure he took my advice. He's a bit of a nutter.'

'He's fine. Stronger than he lets on most times.'

'Listen, just be careful, as always. I'm not at the show tonight, mercifully, so if you need anything, let me know. I'll be here all night.'

'Thanks. I have to get ready to relieve the staff for the evening. I'll call you in the morning. Better still, why don't you and Daniel come to Serge's for lunch tomorrow? My treat, and I'll even sit down with you both and we can have a glass or two.'

'Or a bottle or two.'

'Even better.'

'Chat to you tomorrow.'

'Au revoir.'

This traffic is insane, Pierre thinks driving along Victoria Road, following a long line of cars and vans. 'How can there be so many cars on the road tonight?' He looks out to the black ocean momentarily and allows the darkness to embrace his fears. 'I got a bad feeling.'

Andrew Lloyd-Weber's recent *West End* recording of The Sound of Music is playing in the foyer of The Artscape as Daniel walks in, dressed in khaki cargos, a beautiful crisp white shirt, and black jacket. 'Let's start at the very beginning, a very good place to start,' he finds himself singing along a little bit. *I'm a bit early tonight. That's a first. Time for a nice peppermint tea.*

He sits at a small table, with a number of chairs poorly placed around it, resisting the urge to tidy up the disheveled mess of disorganisation. There are a few other people in the foyer, a handful of well-dressed locals, almost exclusively white and coloured. Like London, the international touring theatre shows in Cape Town are too expensive for most Capetonians to attend. He imagines that Rachel and Ivan will have an opinion about the cost, the cast, the music, and production. He smiles, anticipating the vocabulary to be used.

Rachel finds Daniel at the table smiling to himself, clearly enjoying his own joke. 'A penny for them.'

'Oh, hi, I didn't see you come in. I'm in a world of my own.'
'A moment's peace from the guesthouse, I imagine. Just like me.'
'I was actually thinking what Ivan will have to say about the performance tonight.'
'Well, there had better be an orchestra. Otherwise he will walk out and demand his money back.' She laughs. 'Good of him to organise all the tickets though, and I believe great seats.'
'Can I get you a drink?' Daniel offers as he stands.
'I'll have a glass of bubbles, please.'

Marie strides into the restaurant with purpose, surprised to see so many people. A guy on his own at the table inside the closed French doors of the alcove opposite the bar, a young couple at the back near the open fireplace, and a small group of four in the middle. *Cozy,* she thinks and smiles. She heads straight into the kitchen to check on the staff. Two waitresses are already packed and ready to go. 'We'll miss our taxi if we don't go now,' the youngest of the two declares.
'Go, go, thank you, sorry I'm late. Here, take my scarf, you'll freeze in this weather.'

Annie steps out of the shower, grabs a fluffy white towel, and wraps it around her upper torso. She reaches for her hair towel as William wanders into the bathroom wrestling with his tie. 'For the life of me, after all these years, I still can't get the length right.'
'You don't need a tie tonight. It's not a board meeting; it's a musical,' Annie says as she takes it out of his hand and pulls it through his collar, away from his shirt. 'Much better,' she says as she undoes two of his shirt buttons.
'I only wear a tie so you can take it off me. Do you want to continue with my shirt?'
'We'll be late if you go down that road.'
William winks and heads out of the bathroom.

'And put some pants on,' Annie jokes, 'it's cold outside.'

Still at the Twelve Apostles Hotel on Victoria Drive, Pierre and the rest of the line of traffic have ground to a halt. Clearly there is an accident up ahead, and he remains helpless to do anything about it. He reaches for his phone and tries to call Marie. No answer. He tries Ayden. Also no answer. *Fuck, fuck, fuck!* He thumps the steering wheel.

The prelude starts and Ivan rubs Kris's knee with a level of excitement and trepidation. *I hope to god he likes this.* Next to Kris are Annie and William, and next to Ivan are Rachel and Daniel. The six of them, each with their own expectations and levels of interest in the performance tonight. Perhaps Rachel and Ivan are the most excited. 'At least there's an orchestra,' Daniel says to Ivan leaning in front of Rachel.
'Shh, you don't talk during the overture,' Rachel whispers instructingly.
In any case, Ivan is completely oblivious to anything other than the music and evolving theatre.
The final ascent of the prelude. The stage comes alive with light. An assault of colour, evoking images of the cool mountain countryside. A single character on stage becomes warmly illuminated. 'The hills are alive with the sound of music,' she sings. The audience erupts into applause, which annoys the shit out of Ivan. *For fuck's sake, let the girl sing. Applaud afterward.* However, he is already beginning to be enveloped in the beauty of the set, the lights, the music. He squeezes Kris's knee, turns to look at him and smiles. Kris is clearly enjoying watching Ivan enjoy the spectacle.

Marie stokes the fire with another log. It's drawing beautifully tonight, creating an intimate warmth in the restaurant. She smiles at the couple by the fire, and they ask for two espressos. She moves to the bar to check the POS system. The single guy, still wearing his beanie, with his back to the room, is sitting on a bottle of Chateau de Lille, her imported French pinot from Lorraine. *Interesting.* It was Pierre's suggestion to have something from France on the wine menu, but it is so expensive that locals and tourists never select it. Two dozen bottles have been maturing in her cellar for a number of years now. Pierre checks on them from time to time. As she makes two espressos, she looks at the single guy. He looks homeless from where Marie is standing. Scruffy, worn out linen jacket and mussy, longish grey hair under his beanie. *I hope he can pay.*

The group of four in the centre of the restaurant attracts her attention for the bill. She slips it inside a leather wallet and delivers it to their table enroute to serving the coffee. After they pay and depart, Marie takes a breather and pours herself a glass of sauvignon blanc.

A fierce storm breaks outside.

Lightning silhouettes trees through the windows. Claps of thunder break the silence, suspiciously simultaneously with the lightning.

It's almost real.

'Raindrops on roses and whiskers on kittens,
Bright copper kettles and warm woolen mittens.'

He pours himself a glass of shiraz and sits for a moment in the kitchen. It's been a busy day with a house full of guests, and this evening, after relieving the staff, he had to attend to the duties normally undertaken by Daniel. Not that Ayden minds having to do the turn-down; in fact he would rather be in the guesthouse than be stuck listening to a bunch of thespians prancing around the stage, complaining about the behaviour of a confused but self-righteous nun.

I'll pop in to see Marie later, he thinks. *Maybe the theatre posse might have a drink at Serge's after the debacle.*

Annie links Ivan's arm as they leave the auditorium and head into the foyer. 'What do you think of our Lord Lloyd-Weber's production?'

'It's fantastic. I'm loving every moment of it,' Ivan replies, 'you know, except the 'B' grade songs, particularly that goatherd ditty.'

Annie laughs and pulls Ivan's arm closer to her, almost as if to steady herself walking down the stairs.

'What can I get you to drink?' Ivan asks.

'No need to worry. Bill pre-ordered a couple of bottles of bubbles for the interval when we arrived, and six glasses. So we only need to find where that is.'

'Climb ev'ry mountain, ford ev'ry stream,' Rachel sings, catching up with Ivan and Annie. 'What a show.'

Ivan opens a bottle and starts pouring as Daniel arrives. 'Should I be bothered that the inclusion of black actors is not historically nor geographically correct?'

'Have some bubbles. It will help ease the pain,' Ivan says, handing him the first glass.

Kris and William finally make it to the foyer. 'Best show ever, we both agree,' William says with a wry smile and a wink.

'We really loved that good-night song,' Kris adds, 'I thought it was an instructional song for us. I could have gone home after that one quite happily.'

'Have some bubbles,' Ivan hands them each a glass.

'I think I should. I paid for it.'

They all laugh.

The sound of laughter fills the restaurant, as two guests share a laugh with Marie. 'We've had a fantastic evening, thank you so much. We love your restaurant.'

'It was recommended to us by the man who runs the guesthouse we're staying at… umm Andrew.'

'Ayden.'

'Oh yes, Ayden.'
'Thank you again. I hope we can come back before we head back to Germany.'
The two guests depart in the waiting Uber, which Marie had organised for them. She clears their table, collecting their generous tip from the leather envelope, and keeps an eye on the 'homeless' man drinking the final reserves of the pinot, as she heads into the kitchen.

Finally, Pierre thinks as the traffic starts to move again. He is probably only about 15 minutes away from Serge's. *Keep your cool.*

'Edelweiss, Edelweiss, every morning you greet me,
Small and white, clean and bright, you look happy to meet me.'

Marie comes back into the restaurant, looks at the 'homeless' man, *still there, so not a runner just yet,* then checks on the fire.
'So, my dear Marie, we finally get to meet again,' the man says, turning his face toward her. 'It's been too long, my love. Did you miss me?'

Pierre drives his car as fast as he can maneuver the winding descent down Kloof Nek Road.

'Bless my homeland foreeeeeeee…ver.'
The audience erupts into rapturous applause and jumps to their feet.
Oh, fuckin' sit down. William has had just about enough. He squeezes Annie's knee to show her he's still awake.

Recognising his voice, she is paralysed with fear. Marie can hardly speak. 'How… how did you… f… find me?' She manages to squeeze the words out of her frozen mouth.

He removes his beanie. 'Oh, I've been following you for a number of years now.' His voice is calm and measured. He stands up, and Marie recalls his overbearing stature. 'It's not hard to find the one you love, and what a delight it has been to meet your new friends.' Lucien reaches down below the table and brings out a large box, then another. 'Here, I bought you a couple of gifts. Just something small to say 'I love you'.'

Marie is standing so close to the fire that she feels the material of her dress beginning to scorch her skin, but she is incapable of moving.

Ayden sinks into his favorite chair in the living room and rests his third glass of shiraz on the table next to the chair. He picks up the book he has tried to read for the last two weeks, and within a few minutes he has fallen asleep.

Lucien moves toward Marie with the first box in his hands, his arms demonstrative of his strength, and of the weight of the box. He places it on the table next to the open fire. 'Go ahead, open it,' he instructs, as he heads back to collect the second box, resting it next to the open fire.

Marie retreats, with her back to the corner, keeping her distance from the man who had caused her so much pain and misery for so many years.

'Well, you're probably tired. Let me do it for you.' He walks toward the bar and picks up a knife and inspects the blade above his head. The light of the fire catches the reflective metal and shines in Marie's face. He looks coldly at the knife. 'Of course, I know you like games, my darling, but after you ran off to hide while I was still counting to 100, I knew you would want me to find you, in some bizarre hiding place, in a backward corner of the world.' He brings the knife down and looks at her. His face changes. He smiles. 'But where are my manners?' He puts the knife on the bar and lifts a

chair from under the table nearest the fire, and sets it in front of Marie.
'Please, sit. We have so much catching up to do.'
Marie can't move.
'SIT!' He shouts impatiently, exposing his true colours. He smiles again.
'Please.'

'So long, farewell, auf Wiedersehen, good night.
I hate to go and leave this pretty sight.'
Kris looks at Ivan pleadingly, *please make this end.*

Lucien moves to the front door and locks it. He turns off the lights inside. As
he looks back into the room with his wife sitting next to the fire, her face
glowing in the flickering firelight, he grins, 'Isn't this romantic?' he says. 'As
I was saying,' he picks up the knife from the bar, 'once we had started this
game of 'hide and seek' not even your 'brilliant' half-brother, who, for some
inconceivable, idiotic notion, decided to masquerade as your dim-witted
gay brother, could put me off your trail. Some wine perhaps? You've started
with a sauvignon blanc, I believe. Let me top you up.'

Pierre pulls the car up on the footpath in front of the "no parking" sign. He
jumps out and races toward the restaurant. He bashes at the locked door.
'Marie, it's Pierre. Let me in.'

'And speak of the devil, here he is. What a lucky man I am tonight.' Lucien
finishes pouring a glass of wine in front of Marie, sitting in a chair
semiconscious with fear. He places the bottle behind the bar and makes his
way to the door. 'Welcome, my cunning friend, I've been expecting you.
What are you calling yourself these days? Pierre, right? How French.'

'What are you doing here, you monster? You have to leave us, leave Marie alone. Go back to Paris,' Pierre says with affected authority.

'Such fighting words from the bastard son.' Lucien grabs Pierre's wrist with such strength he almost breaks it. 'Go back to France? And leave my pride and joy, the love of my life, here, in this third-world squalor?' He looks into Pierre's eyes. 'You must be more out of your mind than you pretend to be.'

'I'll call the police.' Pierre whimpers like a child, beginning to unravel. The pain is immense and he can't think straight.

'Now, why would we want more people here? We're going to have some lovely wine and a good chat, then my wife and I are going home… to Paris.' Lucien drags Pierre to the bar and releases him. Pierre grabs his wrist and starts massaging it in a vain attempt to relieve the pain.

Lucien sits at the table opposite Marie, 'Why don't you show Marie and me your expertise in bartending,' he says to Pierre with his eye fixed on Marie's face, 'by opening a nice bottle of Chateau de Lille and bringing us a couple of glasses so we can bid each other au revoir.'

Ayden wakes with a start. *Fuck, what time is it?* He downs the last of the red and heads into the kitchen.

Lucien starts to open the box on the table. 'I see you're still wearing the beautiful ring I bought you in Berlin. That was an enjoyable holiday.'

Lucien pulls out a beautiful bronze sculpture from the opened box, the implication of a bust of a man formed in coral.

'Oh my god,' Marie says, becoming more animated upon seeing the work. 'You bought that from Kris?'

'At your favourite gallery, yes. Nice guy, for a Dutch man. It's for our new apartment in Paris.'

'What have you done to him? Lucien, I can't do this, I can't be with you. You know…'

'PLEASE, don't interrupt me,' Lucien instructs, beginning to lose his cool demeanor. He takes a deep breath, trying to calm himself, but to no avail. 'It was ALL for you, Marie. ALL of it.' He turns his head to the bar. 'Where is that FUCKING wine?'

Ayden pours himself another glass of wine. *I'll call Marie later. No news from Pierre, nor Marie, so I'm guessing everything is normal.* 'Hope those poor souls at the theatre are surviving,' he says as he swigs his wine and smiles.

Pierre brings the opened bottle to the table, together with two glasses. His hands are shaking with fear and rage. He had thought to smash the bottle on Lucien's head, but he knew Lucien better than that. He pours Lucien a full glass, and himself a small amount.

'Pull up a chair and sit with us,' Lucien instructs disinterestedly, randomly pointing at other chairs in the restaurant without looking at them. Pierre obliges.

'So, my darling, and your fabulous, bastard half brother, you get to play another game tonight. I have won the first game, 'hide and seek', and now we play my new game called 'do or die'. The rules are spectac… speectu…' Lucien rubs his face with his hands. 'Spectacularly simple, e'en for you my love.'

Pierre can already see the effects of adding a small amount of ketamine to every bottle of Chateau de Lille less than a month ago, knowing full well that Lucien would be the only human being in Cape Town arrogant enough to buy and drink it. As an extra measure, he added some more in the open bottle tonight.

'The roos… wrooo… rules are, do Paris, or die here.' Lucien starts to look around the room vacantly.

Now is the time to make his move. Pierre stands and throws his wine in Lucien's face.

Marie screams, awakening Lucien.

Lucien turns his head to glare at Pierre, realising he is losing his vision, dexterity, and speech. 'What have you done, you fucking halfwit?'

'Same rules apply for you, Lucien. Do Paris or die here.'

Lucien jumps out of his seat and lunges at Marie. She responds too slowly to avoid his clutch, and falls backward in her chair, with Lucien grabbing her ankle. She screams. Lucien starts crawling over the floor to hold her down as she struggles to free herself.

Pierre, without thinking, grabs the sculpture on the table. It's much heavier than he thought. He throws it in an attempt to hit Lucien, but he misses, instead slamming it into the second box next to the fire, Lucien's second gift, four bottles of butane lighter fluid.

Two bottles smash, spewing butane into the fire and cascading down the fire threshold onto the floor. Flames leap up the chimney and start tracing the flow of liquid into the restaurant. The box and the tablecloth are alight. The flames hungrily trace the liquid through the middle of the restaurant. More tablecloths catch fire. The remaining two bottles explode, shooting accelerant deep into the dining room. Like a released wild animal, the flames leap from table to table, to the bar, climbing up the walls. The ceiling becomes black with smoke.

Pierre can't believe the speed at which the fire is spreading through the restaurant, he stands stupefied for a few seconds, in pure shock. The screams of Marie bring him back to the terrifying reality. 'Marie, Marie?' he shouts, as he falls to the floor to avoid the descending, thickening smoke, to find his sister.

The lights change.

Beautiful, Rachel thinks as a tear rolls down her cheek.

'Climb ev'ry mountain, ford ev'ry stream.'

The sound of the fire is almost deafening. The heat is intense, and the suffocating smoke is starting to invade their lungs.

Each of them can only see the movement of limbs and silhouetted bodies on the floor. It's complete, deadly chaos.

The glass in the restaurant's front french doors smashes. The rush of fresh oxygen invigorates the flames. Outside on Kloof Street, the sound of bottles bursting, of timber crackling, of projectiles racing through the air, floods the cold, quiet street. The restaurant is glowing red.

The sky is ablaze; red, blue, orange, crimson. The family stands on top of the mountain against a glowing backdrop, the most magnificent simulated sunset, as the orchestra reaches the final climax.

The audience jump to their feet, as if each individual had been electrocuted at the same time. The noise is incredible.

Two coughing bodies crawl out of the glowing furnace of devastation, each from different ends of the restaurant, unaware of each other. On Kloof Street, a man, still coughing, staggers to his feet and looks in disbelief at the spectacle, almost wanting to go back in and drag her out. The whine of sirens from fire engines and police cars forces him to run into the dark, cold night.

-§-

Ayden stands in front of the TV the next morning in shock, tears streaming down his face. A young female reporter is standing in front of the charred and smoking remains of his beloved restaurant. His dear friend.

'The scene is of utter devastation. The fire, which is believed to have been caused by a faulty gas valve, completely destroyed the restaurant on the ground floor and the vacant apartment above. Authorities report that one body was found in the restaurant. An identity has not yet been released.'

Epilogue

The leaves, having turned a beautiful shade of rust, are beginning to fall, and the late morning air is cool and fresh. A young waiter, immaculately dressed in black trousers and a clean white shirt, with a white apron wrapped around his petite waist, steps briskly out of the cafe on Avenue George V and toward the table where an attractive lady is seated. Her beautiful long black hair rests perfectly behind her shoulders, and her bright red lipstick complements her radiant face.

'Votre café.'

'Merci.'

She watches as a tall man, wearing a light linen suit over an open-neck white shirt, emerges from the Metro Alma-Marceau. Once she has caught his eye, she waves to him. He walks briskly in her direction.

As he arrives, she stands to greet him. They kiss both cheeks and embrace warmly.

'Bonjour,' he says.

'Good morning.'

'You look happy, Marie. I've not seen you look so well in a long time.'

'I feel like it is all over at last. I have my life back.'

The young waiter returns to the table, 'Un café, monsieur?'

'Oui, un espresso s'il vous plaît.' He returns his attention to Marie. 'How is the apartment?'

'Well, you know that he had great taste,' she points to herself, 'Exhibit A. It's beautiful. And you? How are you, Pierre?'

'Life is good. I'm very happy here.'

They sit in silence for a few moments enjoying the fresh air and the buzz of the city. The waiter returns with Pierre's coffee.

Pierre takes a sip. 'I've noticed you don't wear your beautiful ring anymore. Too many past memories?'

'I took it off in the fire.'

'Ahh.'

'I didn't want anyone associated with Lucien to find me again. So I took it off and put it on his little finger. I left my watch, my heels, and I deliberately left my purse as well. Clearly in vain, given the intensity of the fire.'

'You had told me before that Lucien had passed out.'

'Thanks to you.' She smiles at Pierre. 'He was almost all on top of me, but I managed to roll him off and crawl out of the staff entrance at the back of the kitchen, then I ran down the alley.'

'Clever girl.'

'I feel terrible for my friends in Cape Town. I feel like I should at least contact Ayden. He can keep a secret.'

'Let sleeping dogs lie, Marie. There is no value for either of you.'

They both sip their coffee.

'Come, I promised you lunch. Let's go.'

Pierre stands, drops some coins on the table, and offers Marie his hand as she stands. They walk toward the Pont de l'Alma, stretching over the Seine.